Doctor Who – Ma P9-BIJ-228

DOCTOR WHO
MAWDRYN UNDEAD

Based on the BBC television serial by Peter Grimwade
by arrangement with the British Broadcasting Corporation

PETER GRIMWADE

Number 82 in the
Doctor Who Library

A TARGET BOOK
published by
the Paperback Division of
W. H. ALLEN & Co. PLC

A Target Book
Published in 1983
By the Paperback Division of
W. H. Allen & Co. PLC
44 Hill Street, London W1X 8LB
Reprinted 1984

First published in Great Britain by
W. H. Allen & Co. Ltd 1983

The BBC producer of *Mawdryn Undead* was John Nathan-Turner, the
director was Peter Moffat.

The lines quoted from *The Flying Dutchman* by Richard Wagner,
translated by David Pountey, are reproduced by courtesy of the translator
and John Calder (Publications) Ltd

Phototypeset by Input Typesetting Ltd, London SW19 8DR
Printed and bound in Great Britain by
Anchor Brendon Ltd, Tiptree, Essex

ISBN 0 426 19393 8

'You cannot know or dream just who I am!
But every sea and every ocean, and every
sailor who sails across the world
will know this ship, the terror of the godly:
the "Flying Dutchman" is my name!'
                                    Richard Wagner

For Keith Shand

CONTENTS

1

An Accidental Meeting

Turlough hated it all: the routine, the discipline, the invented traditions and petty snobbery of a minor English public school.

'The Battle of Waterloo', quoted the Headmaster, one day during the boy's first term in the Sixth Form, 'was won on the playing fields of Eton.' And Turlough had screamed with derisive laughter.

Not that Brendon School was exactly Eton College, though it was an imposing enough place. The fine old Queen Anne mansion had hardly changed since the days when it was the country seat of the Mulle-Heskiths, though its circumstances had altered dramatically. Sold in 1922, on the death of old Sir Barrie Mulle-Heskith, the battle had raged fast and furious as to whether Brendon Court should become an independent school for boys or an institution for the criminally insane. Education had triumphed. (Though not noticeably so, it was thought in the village.)

On a fine summer's day in 1983 there was still something quintessentially British about the rolling parkland, from which drifted the sound of a cricket match (all games at Brendon compulsory), and the rose-gardens, arbors and wisteria pergola of the old house (out of bounds to boys and assistant masters) – all of it alien to Turlough.

He longed to escape. But how? He gazed up at the obelisk on the hill above the school – an eccentric memorial to General Rufus Mulle-Heskith. Turlough was curiously drawn to the sombre pinnacle that dominated the horizon, silhouetted against the sky like the sword of some Angel of Death.

'Come on, Turlough! You've got to see the Brig's new car!'

He was startled from his revery by a group of fellow sixth-formers. Ibbotson, the boy who had spoken, presented a sharp contrast to his friend. Whereas Turlough was thin as a willow, his auburn hair, blue eyes and sharp-boned face investing him with an unworldly, pre-Raphaelite appearance, Ibbotson was a lump. It is the misfortune of some boys to be trapped, seemingly for ever, in the blubber and acne of adolescence; just such a one was Ibbotson.

'Hippo?'

The nickname was apt, but not flattering. Turlough's use of it, however, pleased Ibbotson as public evidence of their friendship. And Ibbotson needed friends; because Ibbotson was a bore.

'What car, Hippo?'

'A sixteen-fifty open tourer!'

The object of Ibbotson's admiration was parked behind the main building in the Masters' Car Park. There was something about the vintage Humber, with its immaculate paintwork, polished levers and knobs, and soft luxurious upholstery that gave it a sense of belonging to the old Brendon Court, part of a bygone world of landed wealth and privilege, that made the Minis, the Saabs and the ancient Renault of the other masters seem positively upstart.

2

A group of boys had already gathered around the gleaming vehicle. Ibbotson pushed his way through the crowd. For a moment he gazed in silence, then moved reverently around the old car, caressing the smooth bodywork with his podgy hands, stroking the soft leatherware and fingering the knurled controls, all the while maintaining the most boring commentary.

'You realise, Turlough,' he droned anaesthetically on,' that this car has the same chassis as a 3½-litre Humber Super Snipe.'

Turlough watched him in silence. This was the Ibbotson he loved to mock and ridicule. He felt a stab of pleasure at the possibility of humiliating his friend. 'Crude, heavy and inefficient!' he sneered, genuinely contemptuous of such archaic technology.

'This car is a classic, Turlough!'

'Dull, fat, and ugly – just like you, Hippo!'

The other boys sniggered. Turlough kicked viciously at the bodywork of the car and contemplated kicking the wretched Ibbotson himself.

But Hippo's skin was as thick as the eponymous beast's. Ignoring the jibe, he pulled out a grubby handkerchief from his pocket and set about polishing the scuff from Turlough's shoe, as delicately as if he were tending a flesh wound. He continued his numbing dissertation on the pedigree of the Humber Tourer, waxing eloquent on the lost skills of double-declutching.

It was at this point that Turlough had a wonderful idea. It had the double virtue of embarrassing the pestiferous Ibbotson, and alleviating, if only for a moment, the boredom of his enforced stay at Brendon School. He flung open the door of the car. 'Get in, Hippo!'

Ibbotson was scandalised.

'We're going for a ride.'

3

'Turlough!'

'Come on!'

'We can't.' Ibbotson was stunned by the very idea.

'No one will know.'

'Turlough, we can't!'

'Oh come on, Hippo. Just to the end of the drive.' Turlough sounded so reasonable as he pleaded with the boy. 'You're not afraid, are you?' His voice changed key.

Ibbotson flinched as he felt the cutting edge of Turlough's tongue. 'Turlough!' He made a final attempt to resist the manipulation of his older friend, but Turlough already had him by the arm and was bundling him into the passenger seat.

Despite his acute misgivings, Ibbotson's initial feelings were entirely pleasurable as he sat enthroned on the opulent leather, peering at the ornate dials and gauges.

There was a muted thud as the driver's door slammed shut. Ibbotson turned from his inspection of the dashboard to see Turlough in the driving seat beside him. The older boy tinkered expertly with the timing and turned the self-starter. The engine sprung to life with a dull roar, then settled to a purring tickover which shivered the whole fabric of the car.

Ibbotson was now intoxicated with excitement, as Turlough slipped the old Humber into gear and pulled away with only the slightest scrunching of gravel. The other boys, who had been watching in amazement, gave a cheer. Ibbotson, unused to such adulation, turned and waved like the Queen Mother.

His euphoria was short-lived. While their progress along the drive was as secure as it was stately, on reaching the school gates, far from stopping as he had promised, Turlough accelerated, and turned recklessly onto the main road.

'Hey! you said just to the end of the drive!'

But Turlough was deaf to the protests of his passenger. He eased the car into top gear. The revs of the powerful engine began to build.

'Turlough! You haven't got a licence.'

'So? Who needs a licence?' Turlough revelled in the discomforture of the boy beside him.

'Go back to the school! Please!'

But Turlough pushed down on the accelerator.

Faster and faster they roared along the narrow country lane, Ibbotson gibbering with anxiety, Turlough laughing from sheer exuberance.

'Turlough, slow down!' pleaded Ibbotson.

Turlough accelerated.

'You're on the wrong side of the road!' screamed his friend.

With total disregard for what lay ahead, Turlough turned to relish the terror of his passenger. 'This car's a classic. Isn't that what you said, Hippo?' he shouted mockingly.

'Look out!'

Had he been watching ahead, Turlough would have spotted the van sooner. As Ibbotson cried out, the van driver hooted and Turlough realised he was on the verge of a head-on collision.

The van driver jammed on his brakes, veering sharply to his right, but not in time to avoid giving the Humber a sharp blow, which sent it helplessly out of control, straight towards the hedge.

Turlough was wide awake, confused by the unearthly light that surrounded him. He was floating in an enormous candyfloss of cloud. It was all strangely comfor-

5

ting. Even when he looked down and saw the improbable panorama below, he felt a detached sense of curiosity rather than surprise or alarm.

Turlough looked more closely. There was no doubt about it; the boy lying on the ground below him was undoubtedly himself.

He had a birds-eye view of the field where the car had crashed. He could see it now, half on its side, oil seeping from the broken sump. His body lay a few feet away, unconscious, obviously thrown clear by the impact. Ibbotson stood near-by looking pretty sick, and being talked at by the Head. Trust Ibbotson to escape without a scratch.

He looked further afield. A panda car had pulled up in the lane and a policeman was taking a statement from the van driver. A battered Range Rover screeched to a halt. He recognised the man scrambling out as Doctor Runciman, who hurried across the field to the unconscious figure beside the Humber.

But, if the boy being examined by the school doctor was Turlough, what was *he* – who was also Turlough – doing up in the clouds?

He turned away from the view below. Beside him stood a man in black. 'Who are you?' said Turlough.

'Your Guardian,' said the man.

Turlough looked down once more at the scene below and then again at the stranger. 'What is this place?'

The stranger smiled.

'Am I dead?'

'No,' said the dark stranger.

Turlough thought for a moment. 'I don't think I would really care if I were dead. I hate Earth.'

The man in black smiled again. 'You wish to leave?'

'Is it possible?'

'All things are possible.'

6

'Then get me away from here!'

The man in black, who called himself Guardian of the boy, was well pleased. But there was no love in the smile that he now gave his protégé. 'First we have to discuss terms.'

Turlough could never remember exactly what then transpired in that strange nowhere. He knew only that a terrible pact was made between himself and the man in black, and that when he felt drawn back again to the Earth below and had despaired in his heart at the prospect of life again on that planet, the man who called himself his Guardian had cried out, 'Do you agree?' and he, Turlough, had answered, 'Yes!'

The boy lying unconscious beside the twisted wreckage of the old car groaned.

'He's been lucky,' said Doctor Runciman, turning to the Headmaster as he finished his examination. 'No bones broken. Just slight concussion.'

'It's a wonder they weren't both killed.'

Turlough groaned again.

'He's coming round.'

Turlough opened his eyes. The faces of Doctor Runciman and the Headmaster swam mistily into view. He felt a paralysing sense of doom. He began to mutter deliriously.

'Steady on, old chap. You've had a bit of a knock.'

But it was no fear of Runciman or Mr Sellick that chilled the boy's heart; he had just vowed to kill one of the most evil creatures in the Universe.

As soon as Turlough had been carried to Doctor Runciman's Range Rover and was on his way back to school, the Headmaster turned his attention to the crashed car. 'What's the damage your end, Brigadier?'

Two brogue shoes and legs clad in cavalry twill protruded from under the twisted Humber. Their owner continued his unseen examination of the car, though not without casting certain aspersions on the inmates of Brendon School. 'In thirty years of soldiering I have never encountered such destructive power. . .' There was a glimpse of harris tweed as the speaker began to crawl from under the chassis, '. . . as I have seen displayed in a mere six years of teaching, by the British Schoolboy!' A greying, military figure drew himself up to his full height. 'It's occasions like this that justify the return of capital punishment,' growled the old soldier.

It was Brigadier Lethbridge-Stewart.

2

A New Enemy

To the boys of Brendon School, the Brigadier was just
part of the fixtures and fittings, like Matron's dreaded
cascara or the Headmaster's smelly Dobermann. They
knew nothing of his distinguished career with UNIT,
the top-secret security organisation, and would
certainly have been amazed, had they known, that the
blimpish but kindly assistant master was for many years
the friend and colleague of a Time Lord from Gallifrey.

It was a long time now since the Doctor and the
Brigadier had met. Yet, on that summer's day in 1983,
there was one thing that united them. While, at
Brendon School, the Brigadier surveyed the wreckage
of his beloved Humber, far out in space the Doctor
was assessing the damage to a broken-down TARDIS
(of which he was equally fond).

Without warning a savage and unfamiliar alarm had
sounded on the console, at which moment all temporal
and spatial progress had come to a shuddering halt.

Tegan and Nyssa picked themselves up from the
corner of the control room where they had been thrown
by the violence of the emergency stop. They both felt
in need of reassurance after the sudden jolting, but
there was no point in talking to the Doctor – already

9

at work on the console – as the continuing shriek of the claxon made communication impossible.

The silence, when the alarm was finally switched off, was a relief in itself. The Doctor turned from the systems panel. 'Warp ellipse cut-out,' he announced casually, and began to pull the whole circuit board apart.

The news meant very little to Tegan, who wondered if it was a polite way of saying they had run out of petrol.

Nyssa understood more of the Doctor's technical jargon. She leaned over his shoulder. 'That would mean we were near an object in a fixed orbit in time as well as space.'

The Doctor didn't answer, but continued to make a rough and ready modification of the circuit.

Nyssa watched suspiciously. 'Doctor, you're short-circuiting the cut-out.'

'The sounding of the alarm was a pure malfunction.'

'Suppose there was a ship on collision course with the TARDIS!'

'A ship in a warp ellipse?' The Doctor moved to the navigational controls. 'Do you know what the statistical chances of that are?'

'Several billion to one.'

'Precisely.' The Doctor completed the resetting of the co-ordinates and the column began to rise and fall. They were under way again.

Tegan had overheard enough of the conversation to be thoroughly alarmed. As she saw it, they were going the wrong way down a motorway on the optimistic assumtion there was no other traffic. 'But if there's even a chance of one of those ships on a collision course. . .'

The Doctor interrupted her impatiently. 'There's a

chance of anything!' Did the wretched girl expect him to hang about some crossroads in space, simply because a redundant alarm had accidentally gone off? The type of vessel it was designed to detect had never ever been built – well not so far as he knew. But, seeing the hurt and anxious look on Tegan's face, he smiled reassuringly. 'Statistically speaking, if you gave typewriters to a treeful of monkeys, they'd eventually produce the words of William Shakespeare.'

Nyssa had been watching the empty starfield on the scanner screen, and was perturbed by a dull red glow that appeared in the far distance. She cried out.

But the Doctor was busy lecturing Tegan. 'Now you and I know, that at the end of the millenium those monkeys will still be tapping out gibberish. . . .'

'Doctor!' Nyssa was staring, horror-struck, at the screen. The red glow was brighter, closer, and had taken on a very solid shape. 'Something's coming straight for us!'

The Doctor and Tegan spun round. Out of the void of space a blood-red ship loomed towards them.

The Doctor hurled himself at the console.

'We've got to get out of the way!' yelled Tegan.

'We can't!' cried the Doctor, desperately wrestling with the controls. 'We've converged with a warp ellipse.'

The impossible had happened; forces beyond the control of the TARDIS's navigational system impelled them towards a fatal impact with the on-coming ship. The scanner flared a violent crimson as the vessel filled the whole screen.'

Tegan screamed. 'We're going to crash!'

'Hold tight! I'm trying to materialise on board.'

The TARDIS vibrated to the point of disintegration.

11

The two girls gripped the side of the console in terror. Tegan closed her eyes.

She opened them again as she felt the shaking die away. She noticed that the red vessel had gone from the screen. A gloomy interior presented itself to the scanner.

'Just made it,' said the Doctor rather shakily.

Tegan thought back to the Doctor's parable of the typewriters. 'Seems as if a monkey has just written *Hamlet*!' she muttered sarcastically.

In the sick-bay of Brendon School, Miss Cassidy, the Matron, ruled supreme.

'Right, into bed with you, young man.'

Turlough viewed the iron-framed beds on either side of the sterile, unfriendly room. On one, the starched sheets had been folded back ready for the injured boy. 'Matron, I'm perfectly all right.'

'Mild concussion and shock. You heard what Doctor Runciman said.'

Turlough had no intention of submitting to the dictatorial old harridan. 'I'm not going to bed.'

Matron regarded the boy as a Sergeant-Major might some young recruit who has just said he would really rather not get his hair cut. Nor would her voice have been out of place on the parade ground. 'Just for once, Turlough, you can do as you're told. You're in enough hot water already.' She marched him smartly to the waiting bed.

Turlough conceded defeat, and slipped between the bedclothes. He shivered at the touch of the cold, unwelcoming sheets and looked in dismay round the empty room. He felt trapped.

Then he saw the crystal on the bedside table. 'Where did this come from?'

Matron looked up from where she was tidying Turlough's clothes. 'It was in your jacket pocket – and that was in a fine old mess, I don't mind telling you.'

Turlough picked up the cube to examine it more closely; then dropped it furtively behind the water jug. The Headmaster had come into the sick-bay.

Mr Sellick looked unenthusiastically at the reclining Turlough. 'Well, Turlough, how are you feeling?'

'Much better thank you, sir.'

'Which is more than the Brigadier can say about his car.'

Turlough closed his eyes at the laboured sarcasm.

The Headmaster peered at the sullen, uncooperative boy. 'I don't understand you, Turlough. You make no effort in games. You refuse to join the CCF. You do little work in class – though you've got a first-class mind. And now this!' A look of weary disgust passed across his face, as if Sally, the Dobermann, had just disgraced herself in the drawing room.

Turlough gazed at the ceiling, and wondered if he could really despise the Headmaster more than Canon Whitstable, the school Chaplain.

The Headmaster droned on with a catalogue of Turlough's inadequacies.

'I wasn't driving, you know.'

'What?' The Headmaster stammered to a halt, like a speaker forced to abandon a prepared text.

'The Brigadier's car.'

'But Ibbotson said . . .'

'I didn't want Ibbotson to get into trouble.'

The Headmaster looked curiously at Turlough.

'I went along in case he got hurt. I knew he wasn't really able to drive the car.'

'I see.'

The Headmaster didn't see at all. He was thoroughly

confused. Could it be that some of the values of Brendon School had rubbed off on this sixth-form dissident? It was unlike Turlough to take the rap for someone else; but Turlough was a very unlikely boy.

Turlough stared at the Headmaster. The Headmaster found himself unable to turn away from those cold, clear, blue eyes. There was certainly something quite remarkable about. . .

'Turlough must get some sleep, Headmaster.'

'Of course, Matron. I'll look in again later.'

Miss Cassidy escorted the Headmaster from the room, and, with a last glance at the recumbent boy, closed the door.

Turlough instantly sat up, leaned across the table, and picked up the cube.

It was geometrically perfect and made of some immensely hard, crystalline substance, not of the Earth nor any other planet with which he was familiar. It was as clear as water from a mountain stream and refracted the cold light of the room most strangely.

As he gazed into the icy transulence, he found himself trembling. Something had invaded his consciousness. He could see an immense white cloud. Then he remembered when he had been himself, but beyond himself. 'I thought it was just a dream,' he murmured, half in wonder, half in fear.

He felt a strong current thrill through his body. No longer inert, the cube began to glow until the whole room was suffused with light.

From somewhere beyond space and time a great voice spoke. 'Waking or sleeping. I shall be with you . . . until our business is concluded.'

And Turlough remembered the man in black, and the terrible bargain that had been made. He nerved himself to speak. 'Why can't *you* destroy this Doctor?'

'I cannot be involved,' came the Olympian voice of the dark stranger who called himself Turlough's Guardian. 'I may not be seen to act in this matter.'

Turlough recoiled at the thought of murder, but he was desperate to escape from Earth. He challenged the stranger. 'Why am I still here?'

'Patience, Turlough,' the voice replied. 'Already the elements of chance are ranged against the Doctor. Soon he will be separated from the TARDIS, and in your power!'

Slowly, the Doctor opened the door of the TARDIS and peered out. A long gloomy corridor stretched in front of him. He stepped from the police box followed by Tegan and Nyssa. As their eyes grew accustomed to the dim light, they looked round in amazement at the ship inside which they had materialised.

The companionway ahead of them was paved with marble, the walls panelled in onyx and lapis lazuli. To one side spiralled a grand staircase of polished gypsum, above which hung a great chandelier. Everywhere there were frescoes, mosaics and rich tapestries, delicate objects of porphyry and alabaster. It was like no vessel they had seen before.

They walked cautiously forward, anxious to prevent their feet from clattering on the hard floor.

'No sign of any passengers,' observed Nyssa.

'They're probably having cocktails with the Captain,' joked Tegan nervously.

'What?'

'I mean it's more like the *Queen Mary* than a spaceship'.

They were whispering, like children from the village who had wandered, uninvited, into the Big House. But

15

no starched parlour maid rushed forward to ask them their business.

Another marbled avenue stretched before them, either side flanked by elegant columns. The light, like shafts of autumn sun, reflected ruby and gold in the rich inlaid stones of the pavement.

All three felt ill at ease and overcome with claustrophobia, as if buried alive in the funeral splendour of Tutankhamun's tomb.

'I take it back,' said Tegan, unnerved by the absence of any crew. 'This isn't the *Queen Mary*. It's the *Marie Celeste*.'

Leaving the main ambulatory, they found themselves in a gallery which ran parallel with the main corridor. Exotic pictures covered the walls: fearsome, convoluted abstracts; alien, infernal landscapes.

'You'd have thought on a long voyage they'd want something more cheerful,' remarked Tegan, who knew what she liked, and had no taste for such fantasmagoria.

The Doctor left the girls behind, and, reaching the end of the corridor, passed through an archway into a crescent-shaped gallery. As he crossed the threshold a sudden light shone on eight recessed panels. In each panel could be seen the likeness of a strange being, half human, half alien. The consistory of faces seemed to hold the Doctor in cross-examination. He felt absurdly disquieted and stepped swiftly backwards, away from their gaze. The light extinguished.

From another quarter there came the strains of mysterious music. A seductive symmetry of sound the Doctor had never heard before. He retraced his way between the gilded columns and into another arcade, where he rejoined Tegan and Nyssa, who had accidentally activated the machine that produced this amazing

16

music of the spheres. All three listened for several minutes, spellbound.

At last Nyssa spoke. 'Everything in this ship is designed for pleasure.' There was a hint of Calvanistic disapproval in her voice.

The Doctor was less surprised by such lavish comfort. He alone knew the implications of a vessel which he had believed, till now, existed only in the imagination of engineers and storytellers. 'A ship in a warp ellipse would be travelling for a very long time,' he explained.

The girls shivered as they speculated on the history of the ghostly red craft.

'It could travel', added the Doctor sombrely, 'throughout infinity.'

A penitent Ibbotson stood, head bowed low, in the Headmaster's study. His delight at driving in the Brigadier's car, which had so swiftly turned to terror at Turlough's recklessness, then to relief at his miraculous escape, had become sheer funk in front of Mr Sellick.

'You realise, Ibbotson, that what you did was a criminal offence.' Chastising Ibbotson, the Headmaster felt none of the unease he had experienced with Turlough. 'If it wasn't for the good name of the school, I'd hand you both over to the police. I shall be writing to your parents, needless to say.'

Ibbotson stumbled out into the corridor, tears of mortification pricking at his eyes – straight into the arms of the Brigadier.

'Ah, Ibbotson! And what have you got to say for yourself?'

'Please, sir, I'm sorry, sir. It wasn't my fault. Honestly. I'm very sorry, sir. . .' He fled down the corridor like a terrified rabbit.

The Brigadier, who was a kind man at heart, wished that he had been a little less brusque, but he concealed his sympathy from the Headmaster, who emerged at that moment from his study. 'I trust you flogged that young man within an inch of his life,' he blustered.

'Thank you, Brigadier. I think we should wait until Turlough has recovered before we take any disciplinary action.'

The Brigadier grunted.

'I'm sure you'll agree, we must do what's best for the school.'

'If you say so, Headmaster,' said the Brigadier, thinking of his no-claims bonus. 'Mind you,' he continued, as they walked down the corridor together, 'we can't really take it out on Ibbotson. He was led into this by Turlough. Got a rotten one there.'

The Headmaster was silent for a moment, remembering those cold, penetrating eyes. 'I'm not so sure. I've had a word with Turlough. His story is that he went along to protect Ibbotson.'

'Cunning as a fox. You don't believe him, of course.'

'I don't know. But I'd be reluctant to jeopardise the boy's future.'

'Have you spoken to his parents?'

'I thought you knew. They're dead. I deal with a solicitor in London. A very strange man he is too.'

Ibbotson looked round to make sure that the coast was clear, then quietly opened the sick-bay door.

Turlough heard his friend come in, but continued to stare vacantly at the ceiling.

'Are you awake, Turlough?'

'What do you want?'

Ibbotson had no clearly defined reason for the visit, but in his wretchedness needed to talk to *somebody*.

18

'The Head's going to write to my parents. The police may be called in to investigate. We could be expelled,' he blurted out.

Turlough smiled. 'It's all right, Hippo. I explained to Mr Sellick. I told him it was all my fault.'

'I say, did you really!'

Turlough grinned maliciously. 'So you won't get the boot. Just beaten I expect.' He laughed at the look of dismay on Ibbotson's face.

'They'll beat *you* when you're better.'

'Oh no they won't!' Turlough threw back the bed-clothes, swung his legs to the floor, and stood up fully dressed.

'You can't get up till Doctor Runciman says so!'

Turlough opened the door. 'Goodbye, Hippo.'

Ibbotson's heart sank. His only friend was abandoning him. 'Turlough, you can't leave me on my own!' he pleaded.

Turlough lingered in the doorway.

'Please, Turlough!'

An idea occured to the older boy. The company of Ibbotson might prove reassuring – or at least a source of amusement.

Turlough looked at Ibbotson. He didn't speak. But his eyes said, 'Follow me if you dare!'

Ibbotson followed Turlough down the passage behind the Seniors' Dormitory, past Matron's sitting-room, and onto the landing at the top of the fire escape. Turlough moved as anxiously as the more timorous Ibbotson; to be discovered now would be disastrous.

The coast was clear. With a terrible clatter they ran down the metal stairs. They reached the bottom and hugged the wall, panting nervously. So far so good.

A quick dash across the gravel, over the lawn, and

a line of tall privet hid them from the school. Turlough stopped running. Ibbotson caught up and walked beside him, too out of breath to speak. Together they skirted the willows at the end of the lake.

They came to the hill. A steep path led upward between the trees to where, on the summit, they could see the obelisk.

For a moment Turlough stood and gazed at the distant monument, then without a word began to climb the path.

'Turlough!' called Ibbotson. 'Where are we going?'

Turlough didn't even glance over his shoulder. Desperate not to be left behind, Ibbotson scrambled after his friend, who seemed to have forgotten the other boy as he dashed up the hill.

'Turlough, wait!' Ibbotson had a stitch in his side and his legs ached. He stood gasping for breath, the sweat pouring down his face.

Turlough had a lead of some hundred yards as he disappeared into the trees that ringed the crown of the hill.

'Turlough!' Ibbotson forced himself to go on.

He reached the wood and looked round for his friend, calling out as he walked between the trees.

The first thing Ibbotson noticed was the light. There was no way the sun could penetrate the canopy of leaves, yet the base of the oak tree ahead was brilliantly illuminated. Ibbotson stood still, frightened by the strange aurora. Then he saw Turlough.

The other boy was standing beside the trunk of the tree, his hands cupped and raised above his head, as if in some pagan rite. Ibbotson felt like an intruder, but his curiosity urged him forward. As he drew closer he realised that his friend's outstretched arms were at the centre of the unnatural radiance. He became aware

20

that Turlough's lips were moving, as if in conversation with an unseen person.

'Turlough, what's happening! Who are you talking to?' he called – and instantly regretted his impetuosity.

The light went out. Turlough, who had been oblivious of his friend's approach, wheeled round, startled and guilty. As he turned, Ibbotson thought he glimpsed a small, square fragment of glass that Turlough slipped quickly into his pocket, before dashing off in the direction of the obelisk.

'Turlough! Wait for me!' Ibbotson stumbled through the thick compost of leaves and out into the small clearing on the summit. He blinked owlishly in the sunlight.

Turlough stood lazily beside the base of the obelisk. As Ibbotson walked towards him, the older boy smiled casually as if the two of them had just met at a bus stop.

'Now what?' said Ibbotson

'We wait,' said Turlough.

Both Tegan and Nyssa disliked the cloying sumptuousness of the alien ship. The Doctor, though he had said nothing to the girls, was equally disturbed by the stifling splendour. Yet he continued to explore.

A narrow gangway led from a short flight of stairs into a wide gallery. Though the ornate style of the rest of the ship was still much in evidence, this area had a more functional aspect than elsewhere.

'The control centre,' observed Nyssa, as she joined the Doctor who was already examining a large panel in the centre of the room.

'Could you fly this thing?' asked Tegan.

But the Doctor was far too interested in the controls.

'You don't fly a ship like this.' Nyssa turned from a bank of computer screens. 'It's in perpetual orbit.'

'Amazing,' muttered the Doctor. He pointed to an indicator on the desk. 'This ship has been in orbit nearly three thousand years.'

'No wonder there's no one on board.' Tegan grinned, though she felt repulsed at the idea of being part of a flying mausoleum.

'Doctor, come and look at this!' Nyssa had wandered over to a recess in the far corner of the room. Tegan followed the Doctor across, but she couldn't understand the interest of the other two. After all, the alcove they were examining with such enthusiasm was entirely empty.

'A transmat terminal' explained the Doctor, examining the computer keyboard on the wall.

'And in the transmit mode,' added Nyssa.

'Perhaps the crew escaped in the life-raft,' Tegan joined in nervously. She didn't like the idea of particle transmission one little bit. Like travelling in a food-mixer. She had visions of coming out as taramosalata. Not that they'd ever get her in one of those things.

But, like a 36 bus, the thing was curiously non available.

'Someone left the ship in the capsule about six years ago.' The Doctor had begun to make sense of the complex navigational data.

'Where to?'

The Doctor smiled and turned back to the keyboard. He swiftly converted Tegan's question into language the computer could understand.

Back came the answer.

'Earth!' The Doctor read the information from the display. 'The ship's orbit takes it in range for seven years.'

22

'If the seven years are up, someone might come back.' Tegan looked anxiously at a red light that had started to flash in the terminal bay.

'Any time,' agreed the Doctor. 'I think we ought to get back to the TARDIS.' There was no mistaking the sudden urgency in his voice.

Turlough and Ibbotson stood silently beside the obelisk. Turlough was nervous, afraid of yet another disappointment. Perhaps it had all been an illusion. His fingers tightened round the nugget of crystal in his jacket pocket; that was real enough.

He looked around him. There was a splendid view over the tops of the trees into the valley below; the sun dappling the lake; the old house seeming to doze in the afternoon warmth; the distant pirouette of white-flannelled boys on the cricket pitch. How typical of the Earth – of England! So complacently pastoral! Hardly the time and place for acts of destiny.

Little did Turlough know about the terrible plan of which he was the merest part; a final solution, after which the light would be turned into darkness, evil become good and good be evil.

Nor did he realise that at that very moment, out in space but within transmat range of the obelisk, the Doctor, to satisfy his companions' curiosity, had activated the search-and-reveal programme in the control centre of the red ship.

As the location of the transmat capsule was beamed back from Earth to the ship, so the camouflage circuit cut out. Ibbotson gasped as a gleaming silver sphere materialised between the trees.

Turlough smiled.

Ibbotson stared in amazement. 'What is it?' he stammered.

'Don't you recognise a transmat capsule when you see one?' Turlough walked confidently to the shining globe. A segment slid back to reveal a door.

Ibbotson stood petrified. 'Keep back!' he yelled.

Turlough continued towards the dark cleft in the side of the sphere.

'Turlough!'

As Turlough stepped through the opening, the panel slid back, enclosing the boy. Ibbotson watched, sick with horror.

Then the sphere vanished.

Ibbotson blinked. He rushed forward to the space between the trees, but there was no sign of the sphere – or of Turlough.

He began to tremble. A wave of blind panic surged over him and he dashed off down the hill as fast as his legs would carry him.

Brigadier Lethbridge-Stewart had been to look at his car in the local garage. It had been like visiting a loved one in an ill-equipped cottage hopsital. He suspected the old girl was not getting the treatment she needed, and there had been sharp words with the mechanic, followed by a long and acrimonious conversation with his insurance company. The Brigadier was not in the best of humour as he strode back to the school.

'Sir!' A plaintif cry came from across the meadow. 'Sir! Sir!' It sounded like a small animal in distress.

The Brigadier turned. It was in fact quite a large animal that came tearing towards him over the grass. The Brigadier had never seen Ibbotson run before.

The boy staggered to a halt drawing in great lungfuls of air. 'It's Turlough, sir!' He swayed dizzily. The Brigadier grabbed him by the shoulders.

'We were on the hill, sir. . .'

24

'What?' snapped the Brigadier. Turlough had no right to have left the sick bay. He would be for the high jump this time.

'There was this great silver ball!'

The Brigadier snorted.

'Turlough went inside and disappeared.'

Brigadier Lethbridge-Stewart took a deep breath, about to explain that he had not just arrived on a banana boat, when he saw the tears in Ibbotson's eyes. The boy was shaking like a leaf. Perhaps there had been a genuine accident.

It was tough going, climbing to the obelisk, and the Brigadier was glad to rest for a moment while a flagging Ibbotson caught up. 'If you took more exercise,' he bellowed at the boy, trying to conceal his own puffing and blowing, 'not only would your body be less disgusting, but you'd enjoy a healthier imagination.'

'I didn't imagine it, sir!'

'Take it from me,' the Brigadier growled. 'A solid object can't just dematerialise.'

'The TARDIS won't dematerialise!' The Doctor wriggled inside the control console of his time-machine and scanned the components for malfunction with as much care as Lethbridge-Stewart had tended his ancient Humber. Above him, the column bumped and struggled like a worn-out beam engine, to the accompaniment of another ear-splitting alarm.

The Doctor crawled out from the console and re-entered the co-ordinates. But still the TARDIS refused to leave the ship.

Unlike the Doctor and his companions, Turlough was delighted to be aboard the ghostly spacecraft. As he stepped from the transmat capsule, he surveyed the control centre as if it were the promised land.

He ran to the operations panel. The controls were unfamiliar, but he would soon get the hang of them.

He winced with sudden pain and his hand went to his side – there was something hard and burning in his pocket. The cube was glowing angrily as he took it out.

'Turlough!' came the voice of the dark stranger. 'The controls of this vessel are of no interest to you?'

'But it's a ship! I can get home!'

The crystal flared and the voice of the man in black grew more intransigent. 'I did not bring you here so that you could return home. Your concern is with the Doctor.'

But Turlough would not be held back now. In his impatience he felt strong enough to destroy the importunate old man. He raised his hand to dash the crystal against the hard floor.

He screamed. A terrible force issued from the cube, which seered his arm and tormented every nerve in his body. He writhed and twisted but could not dislodge the cube from his grasp. From the now-blinding radiance, the stranger burst, like the genie from the lamp.

'You will obey me in all things, Turlough!'

'Let me go.' Turlough cowered like an animal.

'Remember the agreement between us.'

The boy shivered miserably. 'Yes,' he stammered.

'You will seek out the Doctor and destroy him.'

In a tremulous whisper Turlough reaffirmed his allegiance. 'I will seek out the Doctor and destroy him.'

The light faded. The stranger was gone. And Turlough knew that the man who called himself his Guardian was evil.

'Turlough again!' muttered the Headmaster as he stood over the empty bed. It seemed that Lethbridge-Stewart had been right about the boy all along. 'I'm sorry, Headmaster,' said Matron. 'He was missing when I came in with Doctor Runciman. And there's no sign of Ibbotson either.'

'I must talk to the Brigadier.'

'I've already sent a boy round to his quarters. But he's disappeared too.'

'Turlough!' shouted the Brigadier. 'Turlough!' He stamped moodily round the obelisk. Confounded boys, dragging him up this wretched hill. He wouldn't be surprised if it was all some practical joke.

'But sir, there was this sphere. . .'

'Ibbotson!' the Brigadier roared. But he didn't want to bring on one of his turns, so he breathed deeply, as Doctor Runciman had told him to, and marched silently off to search the woods.

It was the sound of grinding machinery that led Turlough to the TARDIS.

He stared at the police box as it struggled to dematerialise. It looked like an Earth object, but appeared to have dimensionally transcendental properties that no one from that planet could ever have designed.

The noise stopped as the machine stabilised. Turlough backed quickly into a dark corner as the door opened. Could the young man who rushed out, followed by two girls, be the Doctor?

'Might have known,' muttered the Doctor to himself, as he rushed, like the White Rabbit, down one of the ship's interminable corridors.

'Where are we going?' Tegan and Nyssa scurried after him, determined not to let the Doctor out of their

27

sight. Had they spared a look behind, they might have seen a thin, pale youth slip out of the shadows and into the TARDIS.

'The transmat beam has been operated. The signal is interfering with the TARDIS.' As soon as they entered the control centre the Doctor made straight for the main systems panel.

'Look!' shouted Nyssa, who had seen the silver sphere in the previously empty recess. 'The capsule has returned.'

Tegan looked nervously round the room and out to the gloomy corridor that led to the rest of the ship. 'If that thing is back there could be somebody on board.'

But no one was listening. Nyssa had joined the Doctor, who was pulling the systems panel apart. 'The transmat signal is supposed to cut out when the capsule completes its journey,' he explained.

'Can you switch it off?'

'I hope so.'

'I hope so too,' added Tegan, peering over Nyssa's shoulder. 'I don't fancy a non-stop mystery tour of the galaxy.'

'Ah!' said the Doctor, with the enthusiasm of a householder who has just discovered extensive dry rot.

'You've found the fault?'

'In a manner of speaking.' He stood up and smiled, rather sheepishly, at the two girls. 'It's on Earth.'

Tegan's face fell.

'Come on,' cried the Doctor. 'Back to the TARDIS.'

Once more they trooped along the ornate walkways of the red ship. Neither Tegan nor Nyssa could see the point of returning to the time-machine since it was trapped by the transmat beam, which could only be switched off by going to Earth . . . in the TARDIS! They dared not ask the answer to the riddle. Neither could bear to think of being trapped forever on the ship.

Turlough was enthralled by the TARDIS control room. As he had suspected, the machine could travel in the fourth dimension.

A desperate idea came into his head. If he could travel in the TARDIS with the Doctor he could voyage back to a time before the dreadful pact with the man in black. He could break free of his bond with the evil stranger, yet still be liberated from Earth.

His head ached suddenly and violently. Perhaps the stranger knew his every thought? The very concept of disobedience must be erased from his mind.

Turlough laboured hard to unthink what had been thought. So great was his concentration that he did not hear the Doctor return.

The Doctor stood in the door of the control room, looking at the pale, frightened intruder. 'Who are you?' he said.

3

An Old Friend

Tegan never knew why the Doctor had swallowed Turlough's unlikely story of how he came to be in the TARDIS. Could it have been intuition? A fatalistic acceptance of the mesh of coincidence that was forming around him? Or was it remorse at the loss of Adric – this sympathy for the strange young man who had broken into his time-machine?

Tegan didn't trust Turlough an inch. As if anyone from Earth would just walk into a transmat capsule! Though Nyssa was quick to point out that that was exactly what she had done when she walked into the Doctor's police box on the Barnet By-pass.

Perhaps, after all, the Doctor was just obsessed with escaping from the confines of the ship. 'All set. Earth 1983.' He finished setting the co-ordinates and moved to the doors.

'Where are you going?' asked Nyssa.

'Earth – via the transmat capsule.'

'Is it safe?'

'It worked one way.' The Doctor smiled at Turlough, then turned back to the girls. 'Once I've disconnected the beam, the TARDIS, with you three on board, should follow me through to Earth.'

'Can I come with you?'

Tegan looked at Nyssa. Why was the boy so keen to stick with the Doctor?

The Doctor turned to Turlough, thought for a moment, then, to the surprise of the two companions, agreed to take the young man with him.

'Good luck!' shouted Nyssa, as the Doctor and Turlough left the TARDIS to go back to the capsule in the control centre.

'See you on Earth,' replied the Doctor confidently.

It was as well for Brigadier Lethbridge-Stewart that he had moved to the woods on the east of the obelisk in his search for Turlough. Had he chosen the other side of the hill, it would have done his health no good at all to have seen a silver sphere materialise between two trees.

The door of the capsule unsealed and the Doctor looked out. It was indeed Earth, and he and the boy appeared to be in one piece – which was a relief; as he observed to Turlough, a badly maintained transmat system could do very nasty things to organic structures.

The small box in the Doctor's hand began to whistle and squeak like an elderly wireless trying to find the Home Service. The Doctor looked pleased with himself; they must be very near the beam transmitter.

As they walked from the trees towards the obelisk, the squawking of the detector grew more and more excited, until the Doctor stopped at the base of the monument. He ran his hands over the stonework and from a cavity withdrew a small canister. This was the device which had stranded the TARDIS on the red ship.

Turlough handed the Doctor the tool-kit he had been

carrying for him. The Doctor selected a small instrument and knelt over the transmitter.

But the canister had no apparent opening, its casing being constructed entirely without welding or seam.

'Brute force, I'm afraid,' said the Doctor, extracting a more robust implement from the kit.

So engrossed was he in his task that he did not hear Turlough's sudden whimper. The boy had developed the most appalling headache. His view of the Doctor misted and blurred. Beads of sweat formed on his forehead, yet he shivered with intense cold. Something was gnawing its way through his skull. The invading genius spoke within him. 'Now boy! Do it now!'

But still Turlough knew that his new-found friend, kneeling so vulnerably on the ground in front of him, was a good man.

'In the name of all that is Evil, the Black Guardian orders you to destroy him now!' The voice resonated inside his head and Turlough was one with the evil stranger.

The boy picked up a boulder and raised it over the unsuspecting Doctor.

The Doctor reeled back, choking from the acrid smoke. The short-circuiting of the energy in the canister had caused a small explosion.

Turlough felt the pain ease, the grip on his mind relax. He stared in embarrassment at the huge rock he was holding, then let it fall to the ground.

The Doctor looked up and grinned. 'Sorry about that.'

Tegan could not for the life of her understand why Nyssa had taken such a liking to that pale and shifty young man. The Doctor, obviously, didn't trust

Turlough out of his sight, or he wouldn't have taken him to Earth in the capsule.

Nyssa couldn't agree; but their argument was cut short as the TARDIS column grunted and jerked, then began a reassuringly regular rise and fall.

'Here we go!'

They were on their way to join the Doctor on Earth – out of the warp ellipse and away from that depressing red ship.

At least the explosion in the canister had cut out the beam that inhibited the TARDIS.

The Doctor stood up and looked hopefully about the obelisk. Nothing yet. He couldn't have made a mistake with the co-ordinates – or could he?

Was the noise they could both suddenly hear the wind in the trees? There was a pale blue shadow to one side of the obelisk; indubitably the outline of a police box. The groaning protest that accompanied the materialisation was music to the Doctor's ears as he stepped forward to welcome Tegan and Nyssa.

But his hand went towards a door that was not there. Hardly had the time-machine materialised than all trace of it faded away again.

The Doctor prowled round the empty space in total disbelief.

'Could it have been affected by tangential deviation?' asked Turlough in a very matter-of-fact voice.

The Doctor might have replied that this was an impossibly knowledgeable question for an English schoolboy. In fact, he merely informed his companion that there was no question of deviation with a dead reckoning alignment in the co-ordinates.

Turlough nodded sagely. Without the demon within

34

him being alerted, the Doctor now knew that all was not what it seemed with his new assistant.

But the Doctor had no idea what on earth had happened to his time-machine. 'The TARDIS should be *here*!' he shouted petulantly.

As soon as the column had stopped, Nyssa opened the scanner screen. They had a perfect view of the obelisk surrounded by a ring of trees.

'Where's the Doctor?'

Nyssa stared hard at the screen, then checked the controls.

'Nyssa, are you sure this is the right place?'

'It should be. . .'

'Something's wrong, isn't it?'

'I don't know.'

Both girls looked again at the screen. The hillside around the huge monument was deserted.

'I'm sure the Doctor's only wandered off,' said Nyssa sounding very unsure indeed.

The Doctor stood beside the obelisk looking very sorry for himself.

'Have you any idea where the TARDIS is?' asked Turlough.

'Not the remotest.'

'Will your friends be safe?'

'I hope so,' replied the Doctor anxiously, and walked over to the woods to look for the police box there.

Left on his own, Turlough reflected bitterly that barely ten minutes before, he had been far from Earth, aboard a sophisticated ship, with access to a time-machine. Now he was back on his most unfavourite planet; no ship, no TARDIS. He felt cheated.

At least the cube was still in his pocket. He took it

out nervously. It lay in the palm of his hand, a piece of inanimate glass. Turlough felt angry. He did not like being manipulated. 'Well, what do I do now?' he muttered. 'Say something!' he shouted at the inert crystal.

'Turlough!'

Turlough nearly jumped out of his skin as a familiar voice boomed across the hillside. He spun round. The Brigadier was striding towards the obelisk. The Brigadier was evidently not best pleased.

'So there you are, Turlough.'

'Sir?'

Ibbotson came lolloping up behind the Brigadier like an overfed puppy-dog. 'Turlough, what happened? The sphere. . ?'

'Do be quiet, boy!' snapped the Brigadier. He fixed Turlough with a gaze that had withered many a neglectful adjutant. 'You're supposed to be in the sick bay.'

'I was with the Doctor,' said Turlough, without a word of a lie.

'Doctor?' said the Brigadier, testily. 'Doctor Runciman?'

'This Doctor,' replied Turlough, looking over the Brigadier's shoulder to where the Doctor was approaching from the woods.

The Brigadier turned to face the newcomer. The Doctor stopped in his tracks. A grin slowly spread from ear to ear. 'Brigadier!' he exclaimed in amazement.

The Brigadier looked quizically at the Doctor, who held out his hand.

'Brigadier Alistair Gordon Lethbridge-Stewart,' the Doctor continued, hardly able to believe his good fortune, meeting up with such an old friend.

The Brigadier had no wish to shake hands with the

improbable young man in the ridiculous frock-coat. 'Who are you?' he said coldly.

The Doctor looked quite hurt.

Noting this, the old soldier, who was nothing if not a gentleman, smiled politely. 'I'm sorry, Doctor, but if we have met before, it's entirely slipped my memory.'

The Doctor's hand went to his face which was once again wreathed in smiles. 'Of course!' he cried. 'I'd forgotten. Brigadier, I'm into my fourth regeneration.'

The Brigadier's heart sank. They'd tangled with some fanatic – one of those born-again Johnnies by the sound of it. 'Excuse me,' he murmured, as politely as he could manage. 'I've got to get these boys back to school.'

But the Doctor would not let his old colleague from UNIT go so easily. 'What would you say if I told you I was looking for my TARDIS?'

'What on earth's a TARDIS?'

'The police box, Brigadier!' How could the old boy be so obtuse!

'Doctor, I haven't the remotest idea what you're talking about.' Lethbridge-Stewart indicated that the interview was at an end.

The Doctor grabbed him by the arm. 'Brigadier, even if you've forgotten about the TARDIS, surely you remember UNIT?'

'What!' hissed the Brigadier.

'You do?' the Doctor was delighted to have elicited a positive response at last.

'What's UNIT?' piped up Ibbotson.

'The Brigadier and I used to work together,' the Doctor volunteered blithely. 'Its an organisation that. . .' He got no further.

Interposing himself between the Doctor and the two boys, the Brigadier leaned forward and blasted the

Doctor's eardrum with a stentorian whisper. 'Doctor, if you know anything about *that organisation* you will almost certainly have signed the Official Secrets Act!'

'Ah, of course.' The Doctor smiled. This, at least, was more like the old Lethbridge-Stewart.

'Right everybody!' barked the Brigadier. 'We're going back down.'

Ibbotson, delighted to be with his friend again, fell in with Turlough, eager to ply him with questions as soon as the Brigadier was out of earshot.

Turlough looked nervously over his shoulder. Whatever happened, he mustn't lose the Doctor.

He need not have worried. The Brigadier was equally anxious for the Doctor's company; this young fellow could be a serious security risk. 'If you really are from UNIT,' he spoke quietly but firmly to the Doctor, 'we'd better have a little talk in my quarters.'

Nyssa and Tegan shivered beside the deserted obelisk. A rain squall obscured the valley below them. 'Typical English summer,' thought Tegan.

'Doctor,' shouted Nyssa for the umpteenth time.

'There's no one here.'

The rain in the valley suddenly cleared, revealing the path down the hillside. That too was deserted. A shaft of sunlight pierced the clouds, spotlighting a large mansion, far below, at the base of a rainbow.

But no sign of the Doctor.

'Maybe the capsule's malfunctioned.'

Though Nyssa had more confidence in the transmat process than her fellow companion, even she was getting thoroughly nervous – when a silver ball appeared between the two trees in front of them.

The Doctor must have been sheltering from the storm inside the capsule and had operated the camouflage circuit. A door in the side of the sphere opened and the girls rushed forward to welcome him.

They peered inside the capsule. The spacious interior was engineered with the same dimensionally transcendental principles as the TARDIS.

'Doctor!' called Nyssa.

There was no answer from the Doctor or Turlough.

A sour-sweet smell hung in the air, reviving for Tegan a distressing childhood memory – slaughtered cattle on her Uncle's farm; it was the odour of putrification. 'Doctor!' she cried out in alarm.

Something moved, in the shadow of the in-board control console. The two girls stepped forward.

'Doctor!' gasped Tegan.

They stared at the floor unable to speak. The object of their concern lay at their feet – a creature that was neither visibly man nor beast; a lump of transmuted flesh that flexed and groaned.

As they looked closer, Tegan and Nyssa could recognise vestigial limbs, and the outline of a mangled trunk that wept pus through charred clothing. Then, as the deformed boy twisted itself towards them, they gazed upon a face that, though ravaged beyond all recognition, had once been that of a man.

If this was the Doctor, he had paid a terrible price for his journey in the transmat capsule.

A ghastly rattle came from his throat. He was trying to speak. 'Where . . . where am I?'

For a moment the girls were too upset to answer. At last Nyssa found the strength to reply. 'You're on Earth, Doctor. You came in the transmat capsule.'

'Earth?'

'Don't you remember? You followed us through in the TARDIS.'

'TARDIS? TARDIS?' The injured man cried like a soul in purgatory that has glimpsed salvation.

'The TARDIS is outside. We can help you.'

He tried to raise himself up. A palsied hand reached up to the two girls. 'TARDIS!' he cried again, and sank back exhausted.

Tegan and Nyssa knelt beside him. They could hardly hear his desperate whisper.

'Take me . . . take me. . .'

'Doctor?'

'Take me into . . . the TARDIS!'

It was an excruciating journey. Though only a few yards separated the police box from the transmat capsule, it was nearly an hour before the injured man, supported by Tegan and Nyssa, was brought into the control room.

As he passed through the doors, he panted like a creature long starved of air that has just been fed pure oxygen, then sunk to the floor, worn out by the pain of the transfer.

'It's too risky to move him again. Go and find some blankets. We must keep him warm,' cried Tegan.

As Nyssa ran into the corridor, Tegan leaned over the body. 'It's all right, Doctor. You're safe inside the TARDIS.' She felt for his hand to comfort him.

'Something must have happened to the transmat capsule,' said Nyssa, returning with some blankets and an assortment of the Doctor's clothes.

'I told you those things were dangerous,' complained Tegan bitterly as she tried to make the patient comfortable.

'That boy!' cried Nyssa suddenly.

'Turlough!'

In their concern for the Doctor they had both forgotten that he had not gone into the capsule alone.

As Tegan rushed off to search the sphere again, Nyssa knelt beside the injured man who began to regain consciousness.

'Stability not achieved . . . transmat projection destructive . . . stability not achieved.' He rambled on deliriously, then cried out like a child in a bad dream. 'No end! No end!' He swooned again.

Nyssa watched over the body until Tegan returned.

'No sign of Turlough.'

Nyssa was very quiet. She realised the boy had none of the resilience of a Time Lord. She looked gravely at her fellow companion. 'He could have been atomised.'

As they walked through the school grounds the Doctor tried to find out from the Brigadier what had happened since they last met that had caused his old friend to treat him like a complete stranger.

'Is this an undercover operation, Brigadier? I mean I hardly expected to find you at a boys' school.

The Brigadier grunted politely, but no information was forthcoming.

They came to a halt beside a large clapboard shed at the rear of the old stables, which the Doctor assumed to be the scout hut until the Brigadier indicated they should go inside.

'Oh dear,' thought the Doctor. 'Accommodation, Brigadier, for the use of.' That his old friend should have come to this! 'Your quarters?' he asked, in a voice that suggested they had arrived at Buckingham Palace.

His irony was not lost on the Brigadier. 'Perfectly serviceable,' he grumbled, and led the way in.

The Brigadier's hut was hardly the cosy billet the Doctor would have expected of the old soldier. Even before he saw the disarray, he could smell the damp walls, unaired clothes and abandoned washing-up. It was the usual self-imposed squalor of a bachelor brought up to believe that domesticity can only be provided by a servile member of the opposite sex; but very untypical of Lethbridge-Stewart.

The Brigadier had let himself go. He had always been such a stickler for neatness, discipline and apple-pie order; yet the present owner of the hut was untidy, disorganised and a stranger to the vacuum-cleaner.

As the Brigadier busied himself making a cup of tea in the tiny kitchenette, the Doctor picked up a photograph from the cluttered desk. It was his former colleague in full dress uniform. How different the spruce, military figure of a mere eight years ago from the ageing eccentric spooning Typhoo into a cracked teapot.

The Brigadier turned from the gas ring. 'So what's all this about UNIT?'

'Brigadier, I need your help. I've lost the TARDIS.'

'I don't know what the TARDIS is. I've already told you.'

'And you don't remember me?'

'Certainly not. But whoever you are, I can't let you wander round blabbing about classified operations.'

'There's more at stake than a breach of security.' The Doctor abandoned the tone of good-humoured banter. He spoke urgently to his old friend. 'I've lost my TARDIS and you've lost your memory. I'd be surprised if the two events weren't connected.'

The Brigadier glared defiantly. 'Doctor, I am in full possession of all my faculties.' A raw nerve had been touched. 'If I were suffering from amnesia I'd be the first to know about it!' he snapped.

The Doctor said no more until the Brigadier had brought through the tray of tea things and they were sitting together on the sagging horsehair sofa. 'By the way,' he asked casually. 'How's Sergeant Benton these days?'

If the Brigadier wondered how his guest knew about UNIT personnel he didn't say so. 'Left the army in '79,' he replied, equally matter-of-fact. 'Sells second-hand cars somewhere.'

'And Harry Sullivan?'

'Seconded to NATO. Last heard of doing something very hush-hush at Porton Down.'

The tea brewed silently.

'Ever see anything of Jo Grant?' said the Doctor in a vague sort of way.

'What?'

'Jo Grant. My assistant!' The Doctor lobbed the rider like a grenade.

'Jo Grant. . .' muttered the Brigadier, disturbed and confused.

'Sarah Jane?' The Doctor pressed on. 'Liz Shaw you'll remember, of course.'

The Brigadier turned pale. He cradled his head in his hands.

'Are you all right?'

The Brigadier looked up. 'Someone just walked over my grave.'

'Perhaps it was a Cyberman?' The Doctor looked the Brigadier straight in the eye. 'Or a Yeti. . ., *Colonel* Lethbridge-Stewart?'

The Brigadier's eyes glazed over. The Doctor's hypnotic questioning had transported him a million miles from Brendon School. He was a young man again. He felt the adrenalin flow. . .

Danger! Darkness and terrible danger. . . Abominable snowmen in the Underground. Saved from the Yeti by the most peculiar man with a flute. . . Who was this 'Doctor?'

43

Promoted Brigadier. Seconded UNIT. . . Enemy in the sewers – silver things, bionic monsters. Cybermen! Saved again by the Doctor. . .

Not the Doctor, this ageing dandy with the crimped curls and frilly shirt. Can there be two of them? Regeneration? Impossible! But only one Doctor could destroy the Autons. . .

Exterminate! Exterminate! What are they, Doctor? Daleks? No match for UNIT's scientific advisor. . .

Here we go again, Doctor. Is it really you? The clown? The licensed fool? Jelly babies? Thank you, but no. Where's that police box gone to now?

Don't worry, Doctor, we'll deal with that robot. Strike command coming over in four minutes flat.

Alien planet? Don't believe a word of it. That's Cromer out there! Where are you, Doctor? Doctor. . .

The Brigadier opened his eyes. The young man from the obelisk was offering him a cup of tea. Quite a decent fellow really.

'One lump or two?' asked the young man.

'Bless my soul, Doctor,' said the Brigadier, smiling at the latest face. 'You've done it again!'

The girls felt so useless, waiting beside the inert body on the floor of the TARDIS control room.

Tegan could bear it no longer. 'I'm going for help!'

'Where?'

'There's a house in the valley. I'll use their phone.'

'If only we had the zero room.'

'As we haven't, a hospital is the next best thing.' Tegan was already half-way through the doors.

'Take this.' Nyssa felt under the console and withdrew the Doctor's homing device.

'Thanks.' Tegan grabbed the tiny ball. 'I'll be as quick as I can.'

Nyssa walked with her fellow companion to the entrance of the TARDIS and watched her run down the steep path towards the house in the valley below.

No one remained in the control room to observe that the breathing of the injured creature on the floor had become stronger and more regular. No one saw the body stir, a bloodshot eye open and gaze covetously at the TARDIS console.

4

The Alien in the TARDIS

The Headmaster of Brendon School was of the firm
belief that excess of leisure could only lead to an
unhealthy interest in music or the reading of books for
pleasure. Or worse.

Any respite from the classroom, therefore, was likely
to consist of a lecture on the Bren gun from Sergeant-
Major Mobbs, a cross-country run, or a muddy session
of licensed hooliganism on the rugger field. June 7th,
1977, however, was a genuine holiday.

Clifford-Smith, Shand and Greenland Minor were
on their way to the barbecue on Top Field, when what
they saw as they rounded the corner by the tennis
courts stopped them in their tracks. To a boy at
Brendon, a woman was either one's mother or one's
sister. (Both, if possible, to be avoided.) Consequently,
the trio stared at the young lady approaching from the
lake as if she was some ichthyosaurus that had just
crawled out of the water.

Tegan was so out of breath from her dash down the
hill that none of the boys could make head nor tail of
her story, so it was decided that Clifford-Smith should
escort her to the Brigadier.

The Brigadier was terribly upset. What must the Doctor have thought of him? He was also alarmed that such a significant episode of his past should have been blacked out. Perhaps it was connected with the other trouble? He would have to have a word with old Runicman. Meanwhile, he tried hard to conceal his anxiety from his one-time colleague. 'The Doctor and the TARDIS. How could I ever forget!'

'Exactly.'

'What?'

'The mental block. There must be some reason, some trauma. . .'

'The Brigadier felt his hackles rising. The Doctor was starting to sound like one of those confounded shrinks.

'Some shocking experience. Maybe an induced effect?'

The Brigadier's lip curled. 'I don't scare quickly, Doctor. Nor do I succumb easily to brainwashing techniques.'

The Doctor ignored the unaccustomed bitterness in the Brigadier's voice. 'If there was a way of tracing back how far the inhibition goes, you could get some treatment. . .'

Had the Doctor dropped a match in the petrol tank of the old Humber there would not have been a more violent explosion.

'Treatment!' roared the Brigadier. 'Treatment!' He spat the hated word out in disgust. 'There's nothing wrong with me, Doctor!'

'Well, no. . .' stammered the Doctor, quite taken aback.

'A1, always have been!' barked the Brigadier with an intensity that suggested he was trying to communicate with someone on the other side of the lake.

'Absolutely.'

The Brigadier's face twisted with suspicion. 'I suppose you've been talking behind my back with Doctor Runciman?'

'Brigadier. . .'

'There's loyalty for you!' the Brigadier ranted on. 'Well, I'm not taking my leave at the funny farm. Nothing wrong, I tell you. Fit as a fiddle. Always have been!'

The Doctor was deeply affected by his friend's distress and determined to root out the cause of his debilitating paranoia.

The Brigadier noticed the Doctor staring at him. He heard his own angry voice as if belonged to another person. He started his deep breathing exercises.

As swiftly as it had begun, the storm was over.

'Sorry about that, Doctor. Had a bit of bother a while back. Overwork, you know. Doctor Runciman called it a nervous breakdown.'

The Doctor nodded sympathetically.

'Breakdown?' The Brigadier laughed to hide his embarrassment. 'Don't know the meaning of the word. This one goes on till he drops!'

The Brigadier relaxed. He sipped his tea and began to tell the Doctor something of what had happened to himself in the seven years since he had left UNIT. 'Could have retired on my pension. Grown vegetable marrows and died of boredom in a twelve-month. But then this job turned up. Bit of admin, bit of rugger, CO in the school Corps.'

'Do you teach?'

'Mathematics.' He saw the mischievous glint in the Doctor's eye and laughed. 'I know how many beans make five, Doctor. And you don't have to be a Time Lord to cope with the A-level syllabus.'

'Well, Brigadier,' said the Doctor, putting his cup on the table, 'much as I appreciate your company, I've still got to find my TARDIS.'

It was the Brigadier's turn to look sceptical. 'Your TARDIS, Doctor! I never believed it did half the things you claimed.'

'Just at the moment I'd settle for half a TARDIS.' He grew serious. 'I'm very worried about Tegan and Nyssa.'

The Brigadier frowned and the Doctor wondered if he was about to have another turn.

'I knew a Tegan once,' said the Brigadier.

'Tegan's after your time,' the Doctor interrupted. 'She was travelling with me in the TARDIS.'

The Brigadier didn't hear him. He smiled as if cheered by some private thought. 'An attractive girl. Very high-spirited.' The memory, once released, grew stronger. 'Had an Australian accent.'

'What did you say!' The Doctor was galvanised into attention.

'Australian. Yes, it's all coming back. 'The Brigadier grew more confident. 'Tegan Jovanka. That was her name.'

Clifford-Smith led Tegan through the old stable yard. 'Over there.' He pointed at a wooden hut. Chintz curtains hung at the windows and wild roses grew in a tangle round the door. Someone was pruning the briars with a pair of secateurs.

'Excuse me!' called Tegan.

'Hello there.' The man turned. From his military bearing, blazer and regimental tie this must be the Brigadier the boys had said could help her. She was relieved to find he was no Colonel Blimp; quite dashing in fact – handsome even.

'I'm sorry to disturb you, but I'm looking for a Doctor.' Tegan started to pour out her troubles. 'There's been an accident – well a sort of accident. A friend of mine and a boy from the school. . .'

The Brigadier stopped her with a friendly smile. 'I think you'd better come in.' He ushered her through the door.

Tegan entered the room to the strains of the National Anthem. The Brigadier turned off the television.

'Right, sit yourself down, er . . . young lady.'

'The name's Tegan. Tegan Jovanka.'

The Doctor was wild with excitement. 'It is Tegan!' he shouted.

'That's what I said,' muttered the Brigadier, at a loss to understand the Doctor's sudden enthusiasm.

'Your Tegan, my Tegan – the same person!'

'Of course, Doctor,' said the Brigadier, brushing crumbs from his woolly cardigan.

'Tegan, Nyssa, the TARDIS, they're all here!'

'Are they?'

'Or rather, they were. If you see what I mean.'

'Hardly a hundred per cent, Doctor.' Not for a long time had the Brigadier felt quite such an ignoramus; not in fact since his last meeting with the Doctor.

'I must have miscalculated the offset. The TARDIS came through to the right place but the wrong time-zone!'

The bemused Brigadier shook his head. 'You and that TARDIS.'

'Now it's vital you remember exactly what happened.'

The Brigadier sighed. 'It was a long time ago. Surely what's past is. . .'

'Very much in the future,' interrupted the Doctor,

51

raising an admonishing finger as if to send Lethbridge-Stewart to the bottom of the class. 'You never did appreciate the interrelation of time.'

'Not much call for that in the A-level syllabus,' blustered the Brigadier, not used to playing the dunce.

The Doctor tried hard to conceal his impatience. He must not confuse the old boy any further for he needed the help of his UNIT colleague more than ever before. 'Brigadier.' He spoke quietly and slowly. 'You have in your memory the information I need to track down the TARDIS and communicate with Tegan and Nyssa.'

The Brigadier had always enjoyed a good crisis – not to mention the company of a pretty girl. He poured a generous measure of his best malt. 'Now calm down, my dear, and tell me about it in words of one syllable.'

Tegan sipped the whisky and relaxed a little. There was something very reassuring about the man who had just introduced himself as Lethbridge-Stewart; resourceful, unflappable and utterly British (she was reminded for a moment of Captain Stapley, the Concorde pilot); the sort of person you could talk to about the TARDIS and who wouldn't turn a hair.

She took another sip and looked round the room. Everything ship-shape and Bristol Fashion – just like the Brigadier, who was waiting to hear her story.

'A friend of ours and a boy from the school. . .'

'Boy? What boy?'

'Turlough.'

'Turlough?' the Brigadier frowned. 'I don't think we have a Turlough.'

'So the boy was lying all along,' thought Tegan to herself.

'I'm a new boy here myself,' the Brigadier explained,

52

examining a register. 'Trevor, Trumper, Turner . . . definitely no Turlough.'

But whatever the reason for the schoolboy's deception, the Doctor was Tegan's main concern. She had to persuade the Brigadier to organise help. 'They were travelling together when they came down on the hill.'

The Brigadier's attitude changed instantly. 'Came down? Do you mean a plane crash?'

'Well, sort of,' said Tegan, not exactly sure how to explain an arrival by transmat capsule.

'Good Lord, girl. Why didn't you say so before!' Lethbridge-Stewart prepared to leap into action. 'I'll phone through to our local constable. He can co-ordinate the rescue services. . .'

'No!' protested Tegan, feeling a bit like the sorcerer's apprentice. 'It's not like that at all. If we can just get some medical help and go back to the TARDIS. . .' In her anxiety she referred to the machine as casually as if it had been a Mini parked at the end of the drive.

'TARDIS!' exclaimed the Brigadier. 'Did you say TARDIS!'

'Yes, but you don't understand.'

'I think I do, young lady.' He smiled. 'Tell me, Miss Jovanka. This friend of yours, is it by any chance . . . the Doctor?'

It was a very worried Brigadier who sat, blinking miserably at the Doctor. Little by little his friend had teased the remembrance out of him; but the recall gave him no comfort. Now that he could remember the excitement of Tegan's arrival at Brendon, he was the more appalled it could ever have been forgotten.

'Not to worry, Brigadier,' reassured the Doctor. 'A simple protective mechanism of the brain. The important thing is to remember everything now.'

The Brigadier looked grim. 'Doctor, you don't know what you're asking.'

'Something wrong?'

'I've been in some pretty tight corners in my time, but unravelling all this. . .' He was sweating. He felt himself starting to tremble. He was being forced back into the darkness; somewhere ahead was the bottomless pit. 'I just feel we're on the verge of something really appalling.' He struggled to put his foreboding into words. 'I've never been so scared in all my life!'

Turlough was furious. How dare they lock him in the sick bay. How dare his protector allow it. The Black Guardian was not only evil but incompetent. He snatched the cube from his pocket – but the crystal was dead. Perhaps he should transfer his allegiance to the Doctor; but without the TARDIS its owner, too, was surely trapped and unable to help.

Turlough lay back and reviewed the events of the last few hours. He felt as though he had slithered right down one of those snakes in the ludicrous board game played by Earth children. He also felt very tired. He closed his eyes and was soon asleep.

He must have woken up when the Headmaster slipped into the room, though he was too sleepy to remember how their unusually intimate conversation began.

Mr Sellick was certainly a great comfort. 'There's nothing to be afraid of, Turlough, now that you've explained everything to me.'

'Thank you, sir.' It was a weight off Turlough's mind.

'In fact, I'm very heartened you felt able to confide in me like this.' The Headmaster smiled like a Dutch uncle. 'Though I must say, it's a most remarkable story.'

'But what am I to do, sir!'

'It seems to me you're in something of a moral dilemma.'

'Sir?'

'You've accepted a free passage home to your own people, but, to fulfil your part of the bargain, you have to kill this Doctor.'

Turlough thought for a moment. 'But I don't want to kill the Doctor.'

The Headmaster nodded. 'I can see you're in a most invidious position.'

The more he thought about it, the more Turlough felt hard done by. 'Haven't I done enough to separate him from his TARDIS?'

'I take your point, but in your heart of hearts, do you think you've entirely completed your side of the bargain?'

Reluctantly Turlough conceded that he had not. 'Help me, sir!' he pleaded.

'I'm afraid I can only put the problem in perspective.' The Head was like a wise old judge summing up for a simple-minded jury. 'The final choice has got to be yours, Turlough.'

Turlough made up his mind. 'I think I'm pulling out, sir. The Doctor's stranded but what's been done for me? I've been ignored!' A plan was forming in his mind. 'I shall try and escape in the transmat capsule. He can sort out the Doctor for himself from now on.'

The Headmaster walked slowly over to the window and gazed out at the lake. 'Is that your final decision?'

'Yes, sir.'

'Are you absolutely sure?'

'Yes!' replied Turlough defiantly.

He screamed as the Headmaster turned from the

window and was transformed instantly into the Black Guardian.

'Waking, sleeping, you can never escape me, Turlough!'

As Turlough leaped from the bed to the door he felt a tearing sensation, and the hand that reached for the lock passed unfeelingly through the solid material. He looked back at the bed where a boy lay sleeping fitfully. Once more he faced the evil stranger, utterly vulnerable, an astral projection of himself.

'You see, wretched duplicitous child, I know your every innermost thought!' proclaimed the Black Guardian, hovering by the window like a huge bat.

Horrorstruck, Turlough realised that the dark stranger was lodged in his own mind. Every person, every object could be transformed – through his eyes – into the man in black, at the will of his so-called Guardian. It was the evil stranger within him who had impersonated the Headmaster and invaded his dreams to dupe him into revealing his secret intentions. 'Leave me alone,' he begged.

The Black Guardian glided slowly towards the boy. There was no doubting his ruthless, vengeful implacability. 'I invade every particle of your being,' he hissed. 'You will never be free of me until our bond is honoured.'

'The Doctor is a good man!' protested Turlough.

'I am the Black Guardian,' thundered the stranger. 'His good is my evil.'

'No!' screamed Turlough.

'You will absorb my will. You will be consumed with my purpose!' commanded the Black Guardian. 'The Doctor shall be destroyed!'

Turlough knew nothing of the Doctor's combat with the Black Guardian over the Key to Time, or of how he was a mere pawn in the evil creature's game of revenge. He knew only that he was one with the forces of darkness. 'The Doctor shall be destroyed,' he whispered obediently.

The Black Guardian was visible no more and the astral Turlough returned to the sleeping body.

He twisted and turned between the sheets like a wild beast in a snare, then cried out and sat bolt upright, shaking uncontrollably.

The cube rested innocently on the bedside table. Turlough gave it one look, tore back the bedclothes and rushed to the door. It was still locked.

He glanced nervously back at the table. The cube remained inert. He moved swiftly back to the bed, snatched up a blanket and with it smothered the crystal on the table. He hurled the bundle into the furthest corner of the room.

Turlough looked from the locked door to the half-open window. He peered down at the gravel, two stories below, then started to gather up the folded sheets from the spare bed.

The Brigadier was not given to flights of fancy. Indeed the Headmaster's Dobermann was as likely to get up on its hind legs and recite the 'Rhyme of the Ancient Mariner' as Lethbridge-Stewart was to admit to *intimations*.

The Doctor therefore took his friend's untypical premonition very seriously. He, too, was worried by the level of coincidence in what they had encountered. Synchrony across space and time – as if some cosmic influence was controlling their destiny.

But metaphysical speculation would not find the TARDIS for him, and he needed to establish the precise time of the Brigadier's meeting with Tegan.

The old soldier shook his head. 'That's a tall order, Doctor.'

'Don't worry. Just relax. Think yourself back.'

Very gently, the Doctor coaxed the Brigadier across the years to what, for the subject of the Doctor's experiment in regression, was the past, but which for Tegan was very much the present. . .

The Brigadier did not hang about. He explained his plan to Tegan as they left the hut and hurried in the direction of the obelisk. 'We'll get a message to Doctor Runciman. He'll be on Top Field for the bun fight.' Without stopping, he looked round for a suitable emissary.

'A bun fight?' The young Australian had visions of some Brendon School version of the Eton wall game.

'The celebrations,' repeated the Brigadier impatiently.

'What celebrations?'

The Brigadier looked mildly scandalised. 'The Queen's Silver Jubilee, of course.' He spotted a passing boy. 'Powell! I've got a job for you.'

Tegan looked at the Union Jack on the flagpole and the streamers of patriotic bunting. She remembered the music from Saint Paul's.

'Get hold of Doctor Runciman,' the Brigadier briefed the young boy. 'Tell him to bring his gear and meet me by the obelisk.'

The Silver Jubilee? They were in the wrong time-zone! Tegan was appalled.

The Doctor was delighted. The Silver Jubilee! They could pinpoint the date exactly. 'June the seventh 1977. Well done, Brigadier!'

The Brigadier was less enthusiastic. That last regres-

58

sion had taken him dangerously near the edge of the precipice.

'Come on!' shouted the Doctor. There was no time to lose. He needed to return to the transmat capsule.

And so did Turlough.

No one saw the boy as he slid down the rope of knotted sheets, ran across the lawn, past the lake and up the hill to the obelisk.

The Brigadier was not only angry that Turlough had escaped from the sick-bay a second time, but furious to be tied up with school discipline just when the Doctor needed all his help and attention.

'He's trying to get away in the transmat capsule.'

'What's that, Doctor?' The Brigadier paused in his inspection of the empty sick bay.

The Doctor was staring at a piece of glass he had picked up from the corner of the room. 'That is, if he can repair the beam transmitter.' He continued to peer at the cube in his hand.

'Turlough?' The Brigadier frowned. What was it the Doctor knew about that wretched boy? It was time for an explanation.

'No time for explanations,' said the Doctor. 'It could be done, you know. Then I'd never get the TARDIS back!' He pocketed the crystal and rushed from the room.

'He doesn't change,' thought the Brigadier, and followed him obediently.

Brigadier Lethbridge-Stewart was wheezing like a grampus as he climbed back up the hill, while the Doctor strode effortlessly at his side. He consoled himself with the thought that the Doctor was a much younger man.

But it was not his exertions which caused the Brigadier to halt in the middle of the path. It was the strange feeling that he had been there before.

And indeed he had; not just that afternoon with Ibbotson, but six years ago. It was all coming back to him. He had climbed the hill with Tegan in 1977. He remembered examining the Doctor's homing device with which the girl was finding her way back to the TARDIS. He remembered her sudden fear that the wounded man in the TARDIS might not be the Doctor after all. He tried to give an account of his conversation with Tegan as the young Australian rushed back to the obelisk to rejoin Nyssa and comfort the creature in the TARDIS.

The Doctor followed the Brigadier's narrative as impatiently as if it was all happening in the present. 'Tegan is absolutely right!' shouted the Doctor. 'I am not in the TARDIS!'

'Then who is? Or do I mean *was*?' The poor Brigadier was hopelessly confused.

'You tell me!' replied the Doctor, desperate for more news about the other time zone.

Nyssa stood outside the TARDIS looking down into the valley and willing Tegan to return with help. She turned to go back into the control room, reluctant to leave the Doctor on his own.

She entered through the double doors in time to see the injured man stagger to his feet. 'Doctor, you're better!'

He stumbled, and nearly collapsed on the floor again. He grabbed at the side of the console for support, at the same time turning for a better view of the girl in the doorway.

His face had indeed begun to repair, but it was not that of the Doctor. Nyssa stood rooted to the spot.

'Perpetual regeneration,' the injured man muttered to himself, deliriously.

'Regeneration?' Was that what he was trying to say? Regeneration! That would explain everything. Nyssa remembered Pharos and the terrible moment when the Doctor fell from the radio telescope. She remembered how, once before, they had comforted a Time Lord with the face of a stranger. 'Doctor, you don't mean it's happening again?'

He groaned. 'Life without end or form . . . changing . . . changing . . .'

Nyssa had never seen the Doctor so wretched.

He tottered dizzily, and fell forward over the console.'I shall regain strength soon,' he stuttered.

Nyssa could see the wild, staring eyes desperately scanning the instruments.

'My mind is clouded,' he gasped. He focused on the girl. 'You understand the navigation?'

'Well, a bit,' said Nyssa. 'At the moment we're still aligned with the ship,' she added, trying to sound more positive.

'Ah, that is well.' It was as if he grew stronger. 'Prepare to leave at once.'

'We can't leave without Tegan!'

'At once!' he screamed.

'Doctor, you don't know what your saying.'

But he was deaf to her pleading.

'Tegan will be back soon.'

He was leaning over the console, struggling to breathe as Nyssa ran out through the double doors. He saw her leave from the corner of his eye. No matter

– she would be back as soon as the Tegan person arrived, and then the TARDIS would be at his disposition.

How he relished the irony of it: he, Mawdryn, had been mistaken for this Doctor. Now, if the Doctor was the owner of the TARDIS he must be a Time Lord. Mawdryn reflected bitterly how it had been the Time Lords who abandoned him; condemned them all to eternal torment and despair. But now the ending would come.

He started to drag on the heavy red coat that Nyssa had brought with the blankets to keep him warm. He, Mawdryn, would *be* a Time Lord!

It was much safer, Nyssa decided, to wait for Tegan outside the TARDIS. The Doctor, in his half-regenerated state, was a frightening and unpredictable personality. If only Tegan would come back.

'Nyssa!'

To her immense relief, Tegan came running from the trees. 'Quickly!' shouted Nyssa. 'We've got to take off.'

'Nyssa . . . that man in the TARDIS. . .' She paused to get her breath back. 'I don't think he is the Doctor.'

'But he *is*! The transmat process induced a regeneration.'

'What!'

'Don't worry, I know all about regeneration.' The Brigadier, striding purposefully up behind Tegan, spoke like a midwife reassuring a nervous father-to-be. 'I've seen it all before.'

'So have we, and the Doctor almost died.'

'Come on,' said the Brigadier, and disappeared into the TARDIS.

'Who is that person?' asked Nyssa, registering Lethbridge-Stewart for the first time.

'Brigadier Lethbridge-Stewart, of course. Come on!'

The Brigadier stood in the doorway of the control room and smiled; it was good to be on board again.

A figure in a familiar red coat stood watching the screen on the far side of the console.

'Doctor!' The Brigadier held out his hand.

The man in the Doctor's red coat turned slowly. Tegan and Nyssa, running in behind the Brigadier, screamed.

The injured creature from the transmat capsule had recuperated amazingly. But he was nothing like the Doctor as any of them had ever known him, with his bulging reptilian eyes, his high domed forehead and slimy flesh that crept and quivered like a stranded fish.

They confronted an alien.

5

Return to the Ship

It was one of the hottest days of 1983 and the Brigadier was sorely in need of a rest. But the Doctor urged him faster and faster up the hill to the obelisk.

'Don't you see, Brigadier? The TARDIS came to Earth in 1977, and so did the transmat capsule, carrying someone – or something – from the ship in space.'

'And Tegan and the other girl think – or thought – that it was you?'

The Doctor was losing patience. After all, the man had been in contact with Tegan and Nyssa in 1977 when the alien arrived on the first visit to Earth of the transmat capsule. 'You were there, Brigadier!' He spoke as calmly as he could. 'You tell me!'

The Brigadier recoiled, like a child presented with the dentist's drill. 'No, Doctor! Please don't make me remember!'

'You must! I need to know what happened so I can protect Tegan and Nyssa!'

The Brigadier knew he had failed his old colleague. 'Even if I wanted to I couldn't recall any more.' He wished he could explain the inpenetrable barrier that walled off part of his mind.

The Doctor put a friendly arm on his shoulder. 'We

could have reached the cause of your nervous breakdown.'

'Good heavens! Do you think so?'

The Doctor was thinking that an experience which had been traumatic enough to give Brigadier Lethbridge-Stewart a nervous breakdown must have been terrible indeed. 'Come on! We've got to get to the capsule before Turlough works out how to operate it. It's the only way I can contact the TARDIS!'

It was beyond the Brigadier's comprehension how a boy from the sixth form could understand the mechanism of a transmat capsule (whatever that might be). But, what was more to the point, neither did he know how he was going to make it to the top of the hill without collapsing in an undignified heap. He struggled to keep up with the Doctor.

The Doctor could already see Turlough kneeling beside the transmitter. They were just in time. He increased the pace, leaving the asthmatic Brigadier behind him.

Turlough had been relieved to discover that the transmitter was not as badly damaged as he had feared. It would be quite possible to cross-patch one or two back-up circuits, substitute components from the camouflage function for those damaged in the location transmission section and. . .

'Where did you learn about transmat radiology?'

Turlough had been too engrossed to notice the approach of the Doctor who now stood behind him. He spun guiltily round. But the Doctor was already opening his tool-box from which he selected several pieces of equipment.

The Doctor explained how the police box had materialised in the wrong time-zone as he started work on the broken cylinder. Turlough was amazed that anyone should have such an intuitive understanding of the complex microcircuitry and was fascinated by the Doctor's modifications. Of course, he was trying to contact his TARDIS which was within a few yards of where they were standing, but six years in the past. Surely, contact was impossible? And yet. . .

Neither Turlough nor the Doctor noticed a panting Brigadier beside them. In normal circumstances Lethbridge-Stewart would have sent Turlough back to school with a flea in his ear. In fact he said nothing, but stared at the silver sphere between the two trees; it would seem Ibbotson deserved an apology.

Turlough was impressed. The Doctor had arranged for the beam to be reflected off the ship in such a way that, with the warp ellipse absorbing the time differential, it would activate the communications system of the TARDIS in 1977.

'Will it work?' asked the Brigadier bluntly.

'Always the optimist,' sighed the Doctor without looking up.

Turlough grinned. The Doctor went even higher in his estimation.

'By the way, I think this is yours.' The Doctor had been fishing in his pocket for another tool and the crystal cube had fallen to the ground. He picked it up and threw it at Turlough, who caught it as if it were a red-hot coal.

As he stared compulsively into the translucence, he felt a surge of passionate hatred for the young man kneeling in front of the transmitter. *The Doctor must be destroyed*!

'You're not the Doctor!' Tegan challenged the alien in the TARDIS control room.

'You travel with a Time Lord and know nothing of metamorphosis?' Mawdryn was playing a deadly game of bluff. At all costs he must convince the tall Earthman and the two girls that he was the Time Lord.

'It wasn't like this before.' Tegan glared disbelievingly across the console. 'When the Doctor changed, he was human!'

'Is a Gallifreyan human?'

'He was . . . normal!' She looked in disgust at the features of the creature from the capsule.

Mawdryn had nothing but scorn for the purblind Earthwoman. 'What do you know, prattling child, of the endless changing!' he sneered.

'I know that when the Doctor regenerated he didn't turn into an alien.'

'The transmatting induced a mutative catalysis.'

Tegan felt less sure of herself and turned to Nyssa. 'Is that possible?'

'I don't know . . . it could be.'

Tegan appealed to the Brigadier who was as confused as Nyssa. 'I've seen this happen twice before – different each time.' He shook his head, reluctant to believe that such an unattractive creature was the latest incarnation of his old friend. But he had to agree that, logically, it could be the Doctor.

'The condition will remain unstable,' continued Mawdryn. 'The transmutation can be modified, but not in the TARDIS.'

This sounded very plausible to Nyssa who, mistakenly, assumed he was referring to the zero room, the healing central chamber of the TARDIS, that had had to be jettisoned on the way to Castrovalva.

'We return to the ship,' Mawdryn announced.

'The ship? But we can't leave Turlough,' protested Tegan. 'He doesn't belong in this time-zone.'

'Turlough?'

The boy who came with you in the capsule.'

'There was no boy,' replied Mawdryn, irritated at this sudden irrelevance. He instantly regretted such impatience.

His answer made Tegan suspicious. 'If you're the Doctor you should have transmatted to Earth in 1983. This is 1977!' she challenged.

'Any escape from a warp ellipse can cause temporal anomalies,' countered Mawdryn.

'It's true,' whispered Nyssa to Tegan. 'That's what must have happened to the TARDIS.'

Tegan was not in a position to argue and Mawdryn was grateful the Earthchild was as ignorant as she was aggressive. He tried to smile, though such a contortion of his hideous features produced only a frightening leer. 'I need your assistance to return the TARDIS to the ship.' He strove to keep the tension from his voice.

But no one moved to prepare the time machine for dematerialisation. Nyssa, Tegan and the Brigadier were stranded in a no-man's-land of uncertainty, half-believing that the mutated being was the Doctor, desperately in need of their help, and half-convinced that he was a dangerous imposter.

Mawdryn trembled; so much was at stake. If only he could get the TARDIS to the ship. If only the genuine Time Lord would follow in pursuit. He struggled hard to remember the names he had heard the man and the two girls use to each other. 'Tegan! Nyssa! Brigadier! My old friends!' he pleaded. 'Please help me!' He leaned, exhausted, against the console. Tears of frustration flooded his eyes.

Tegan and Nyssa looked helplessly towards the Brigadier, who had already made up his mind. If there was the remotest chance that this fellow was the Doctor, he had to be given the benefit of the doubt.

Nyssa moved to the control panel.

'Do not enter new co-ordinates. Activate sequential regression,' ordered Mawdryn.

Nyssa obeyed. 'We're ready to leave, Brigadier.' She hesitated to close the doors.

'I'm coming with you.'

'But Brigadier. . .'

'Don't argue!' He silenced the two civilians, both of whom were only too glad of his company.'

The double doors were shut, the co-ordinate settings reconfirmed, all checks completed and Nyssa's hand poised over the dematerialisation control, when the drone began. It was a sound they had never heard before.

'Not another alarm?'

'I don't know,' said Nyssa moving round the console. I think it's from the communications system.'

The Doctor stood up, looking rather pleased with himself; the transmitter was working. Already the signal should be reaching the TARDIS. 'Tegan and Nyssa can use the beam as a beacon,' he explained to the Brigadier. 'If all goes well the TARDIS will reappear. . . Oh no!' He stopped. 'Quickly, Brigadier!' He grasped the old soldier by the shoulders. 'Think! Did you go on board the TARDIS with Tegan and Nyssa?'

'I can't remember. Does it really matter?'

'Of course it matters! Can you imagine what would happen if you walked out of the TARDIS in 1977 and met yourself in 1983?'

'That's ridiculous.'

'Not ridiculous, but almost certainly catastrophic.'

'You mean I could be two people?'

'Certainly.' The Doctor tried to impress upon the bemused Brigadier the seriousness of the Blinovitch Limitation Effect. 'You could exist twice over, but because you're basically the same person any close contact would short-circuit the time differential created by the journey in the TARDIS. The energy discharge would be entirely unpredictable.'

The Brigadier struggled hard to remember what had happened when he and Tegan reached the top of the hill in 1977. From the darkness one faint, misty image emerged; a vanishing TARDIS . . . he was left beside the obelisk . . . alone! He tried to explain the distant, curiously upsetting recollection to the Doctor.

Neither of them saw Turlough dart forward to the buzzing transmitter. There was a noise like a firecracker and the Doctor swung round from his conversation with the Brigadier to see a small whisp of smoke over the apparatus. He rushed forward to inspect the damage.

It did not take him long. 'We won't be going to the ship,' he announced.

'The transmitter is useless. I've lost all contact with the TARDIS.'

The Doctor's dismay was nothing to the relief of Mawdryn when the drone in the TARDIS stopped sounding; any communcation from outside would be disastrous to his plans. 'Dematerialise!' He commanded.

Nyssa prepared to obey.

'Wait!' Tegan held back her fellow companion. 'If that sound came from the communications system, someone might be trying to get in touch with us.'

71

The girl was not as stupid as her brashness suggested. Mawdryn's putrid flesh quaked.

'Perhaps it was the Doctor,' added Tegan.

'*I* am the Doctor!' shrieked Mawdryn. 'Dematerialise immediately!'

Nyssa hesitated.

'Time is running out. We must leave this place at once.'

The gentle Nyssa could no longer endure the distress of a man who might be the Doctor. Her hand moved to the lever that would activate the TARDIS.

'No!' Tegan dragged Nyssa away from the console, but already the slow rise and fall had begun.

The journey to the ship did not take long; within minutes of real time, they had entered the warp ellipse and the old police box made a second incongruous appearance inside the sombre vessel.

Nyssa opened the scanner.

'The ship!' cried Mawdryn.

'Is it indeed,' muttered the Brigadier suspiciously. The marble hall he could see on the scanner was not his idea of the inside of a spacecraft.

Mawdryn prepared to leave. 'You will stay in the TARDIS,' he informed the Brigadier and the girls.

Tegan quickly placed herself between Mawdryn and the double doors. 'If you're in a regeneration crisis you'll need all the help you can get.'

'No!' He was surprised at her continuing defiance.

'She's right, Doctor,' said the Brigadier, trying at the same time to show respect for a possible Time Lord, yet still support the plucky Australian.

'I must go into the ship alone.'

Tegan stood her ground. She was not going to let the creature from the transmat capsule out of her sight.

Mawdryn staggered giddily. The atmosphere of the

TARDIS had helped restore his strength, but his conflict with the Earthchild had dissipated that new-found energy. In a weary, broken voice he began to plead with her. 'You do not understand the nature of the transmogrification. The unique restorative condi-tions of that vessel' – he indicated the screen, then turned to his three fellow passengers – 'the presence of other life-forms would inhibit the reparation.'

The Brigadier and Nyssa glanced uncertainly at each other, while Tegan glared implacably at Mawdryn. 'We've all seen the Doctor regenerate before and the evidence suggests that without the presence of other life-forms he could die.'

Mawdryn abandoned reasoned argument. 'Open the doors,' he screamed.

Nyssa moved to the console, but Tegan pulled her out of the way. 'You're not going out into the ship!'

Mawdryn began to groan with pain and rage.

'Either you stay here or we go with you.'

The creature was fighting for air. He clawed and twisted like a drowning cat. Tegan willed herself not to relent, but Nyssa was less resilient. She edged towards the door control lever.

'Nyssa! He could reactivate the beam and the TARDIS would be trapped on the ship for ever.'

'But if he is the Doctor. . .'

'I don't believe it.'

'The doors!' howled Mawdryn.

'No!'

'You are destroying me!' He collapsed exhausted on the floor and began to sob. 'Spare me the endurance of endless time, the torture of perpetuity.' He was now at their mercy. 'For pity's sake, release me!' he begged.

Tegan could hold out no longer. She turned to the

Brigadier. The Brigadier was a professional fighter, but even he could not willingly inflict suffering on a defenceless man. 'Let him go,' he ordered.

Nyssa opened the doors and Mawdryn stumbled out of the TARDIS.

Tegan was trembling from the strain of the confrontation. 'I hope you know what you're doing,' she said quietly.

'Keeping him in the TARDIS might have killed him,' answered the Brigadier.

'And we can't be certain he isn't the Doctor.'

'Can't we?'

They all looked at the scanner to see Mawdryn drag himself from the time machine and merge into the shadows of the alien ship.

The Doctor stood beside the obelisk staring disconsolately down into the valley. Earth was certainly an attractive planet – his favourite in fact – but there is nowhere in the Universe, however beautiful, that does not lose its charms when it becomes a place of exile. 'If only I had some sort of equipment for tracking the TARDIS,' he muttered to himself.

'What you need is a homing device.'

The Doctor smiled sardonically at his old friend. 'Thank you, Brigadier. I forgot you had such a remarkable talent for perceiving the obvious.'

'I have such an object,' observed the Brigadier, as inconsequentially as if he referred to a boy-scout's pocket compass.

'What did you say!'

'Tegan gave it to me.'

'Brigadier that was six years ago. Is it too much to hope that. . .?'

The Brigadier remained infuriatingly unaffected by

the Doctor's excitement. 'Never know when something's going to come in useful.'

'You mean. . .'

'No idea what it was or where it came from.' For the Brigadier, the sudden remembering merely provided an explanation for the glass ball at the bottom of his junk box.

For the Doctor it was the only chance of making contact with his TARDIS. 'Brigadier, where is it?' he shouted, losing all patience.

'Back in the hut.'

The Doctor was already off down the hill. 'Hurry, man. We haven't a moment to lose!'

There were bits of used string, pitted with sealing wax, carefully unravelled and rewound; a broken alarm clock; a button stick; an old penknife; some clothes coupons; a twisted tube of moustache wax; a gas mask; a pair of nut-crackers; a patent self-stropping razor . . . and there at the very bottom of a perfectly useless collection of bits and bobs in the rusty ammunition box: the Doctor's homing device.

The Doctor held it lovingly in his hands. As he made contact with the activator the plaintive bleep brought a boyish grin to his face.

It was a puzzle to the Brigadier how he could so completely have forgotten that on Jubilee Day the same little box of tricks had directed Tegan to the TARDIS on top of the hill.

Once more the sensor was indicating the location of the Doctor's time-machine.

'I should have known.' The Doctor had stopped smiling.

'You've located the TARDIS?' Till then Turlough had been silent.

'It's gone back to the ship.'

The Doctor now had a far clearer picture than the Brigadier of what had happened on 7 June 1977. The wounded creature from the sphere, unable to endure a second journey in the capsule, had needed the TARDIS to return to his ship. Tegan and Nyssa must have gone with him, believing him to be himself – the Doctor.

The Brigadier was equally grim-faced as the Doctor explained the predicament. 'So Tegan and her friend are marooned in space at the mercy of this *thing*.'

The Doctor wondered fearfully what sort of creature his impersonator could be, who voyaged for so long in such a strange ship.

'Travelling in a warp ellipse', he explained to the Brigadier and Turlough, 'is a form of infinity.'

'You make him sound like some kind of Flying Dutchman.'

The Doctor stared at the Brigadier. 'Condemned to sail the Universe for all eternity?' It was an interesting idea.

'Nonsense. No one is immortal. . .' The Brigadier shivered. 'Are they?'

But the Doctor had already turned his attention to getting on board the alien's spacecraft.

'You can't use the capsule!' protested Turlough. 'There's no beam.' If he felt any guilt about the damage to the cylinder, he concealed it from the Doctor.

'You're forgetting this.' The Doctor held up his homing device. 'The TARDIS is on board the ship, and this will home in on the TARDIS.'

The Brigadier groaned. Back to the obelisk again!

Brigadier Lethbridge-Stewart was the last to reach the top of the hill. Helped by Turlough, the Doctor was already installing the homing device in the navigational unit of the transmat capsule as his exhausted friend stumbled breathlessly through the door of the silver sphere. 'This is the third time today I have yomped up this wretched hill!' he grumbled.

The Doctor finished his work. 'Good of you to see me off, Brigadier.'

But Lethbridge-Stewart had no intention of letting the Doctor out of his sight. Heaven knows what trouble the man would get into, left to his own devices.

For reasons far more devious than those of the Brigadier, Turlough was determined to stick with the Doctor as well.

'Don't be ridiculous!' protested the Brigadier, who had had quite enough of the precocious young man for one day.

'The Doctor needs my help.'

The Brigadier grunted. There was no denying it, the boy had remarkable skills. He wondered what Mr Sellick was going to say about it all.

The Doctor closed the capsule door.

'How long will the journey take?' The Brigadier braced himself, expecting at any moment to be blasted off the hill like a cannon ball.

The Doctor opened the door again.

The old soldier blinked as he looked out into the control centre of Mawdryn's ship.

As Mawdryn left the unique atmosphere of the TARDIS he felt the strength go out of him. He clawed at the hard, smooth walls of his ship, but there was no resilience to his limbs. He grasped at a pillar, but on contact with the faceted marble his flesh crumbled like fly-blown fungus. He collapsed slowly to the floor. The Doctor's red coat was already sodden with pus and liquified flesh. Mawdryn moaned at the pain of his dissolution and longed for oblivion. But now he needed the laboratory. He must reach the apparatus. He must go on.

He undulated what remained of his body, and his viscous torso slid slowly forward along the corridor. Every inch of the way was the most appalling agony. He began to fear that time was running out. The girl, Tegan, might take the TARDIS back to Earth, to be reunited with the genuine Time Lord. Never again would there be the chance of an ending. Mawdryn needed help. He turned off the main companionway.

The unearthly faces gazed haughtily down as Mawdryn slithered into the hall of likenesses. He stopped below the central icon that had so disturbed the Doctor on his first exploration of the ship. With a supreme effort of will he raised himself up towards the frame. 'Mawdryn has returned!' he cried. 'It is time for the awakening. Help me!'

But neither help nor answer came.

Fearing that his frail voice had not reached his comrades in the dormition chamber, Mawdryn called more loudly. 'My brothers, awake. Mawdryn has returned. I have brought to our ship a TARDIS. . .' He felt himself weakening. Hope alone gave him the strength to continue. 'The time of our ending is near!' he called.

But the news fell upon deaf ears.

'Help me!' Mawdryn strained again to reach the chamber release, but the effort was beyond him, and with a cry of despair he fell back to the floor.

In the TARDIS control room, the Brigadier, Tegan and Nyssa stared at the screen. There was no sign of any activity in the ship. The Brigadier began to suspect

that Tegan had been right about the 'Doctor'. But he
could never have imagined that the greatest danger,
out there in the ship, was himself; for it would have
been beyond the comprehension of the common-sense
military man in the control room that he could ever
meet up with his own person – some six years older.

'Right!' The Brigadier turned to the doors. 'Time
for a recce. I think we should keep an eye on this
character.'

'I'm coming with you.'

'You girls are staying here.'

'We girls,' bristled Tegan, 'are perfectly capable
of. . .'

'You will both remain in the TARDIS! And that is
an order, Miss Jovanka,' he added as he left the control
room, in case Tegan had forgotten that both Brigadiers
and schoolmasters should be obeyed without question.

'Chauvinist pig!' muttered Tegan under her breath.

'Good Heavens!' muttered the Brigadier as he
stepped out of the TARDIS; he had never seen such
luxury in a ship before.

'Good heavens!' exclaimed an older Lethbridge-
Stewart as he walked with the Doctor and Turlough
along the corridor from the control centre. 'Such
luxury!'

'It's not an ordinary ship, Brigadier.'

The old soldier snorted. Ostentation of this sort did
not meet with his approval.

As they continued into the body of the vessel, the
Brigadier felt a prickling sensation on his wrists and
the back of his neck. Static electricity, he concluded,
without inquiring whether the other two had also
experienced the phenomenon.

He was not to know that his younger self was, at

that same moment, exploring a parallel corridor. As the younger Brigadier moved away into a side passage, the Doctor's gruff companion from 1983 noticed that the tingling had stopped.

So had the Doctor. He looked round as if admiring the décor.

'Doctor, we're supposed to be looking for the TARDIS. Your friends could be in danger.'

The Doctor shook his head. 'The creature will have left the TARDIS. He'll need his own life-support systems.' He continued to examine the walls. 'Somewhere there must be. . .' He caught sight of a small companionway leading off the main corridor. 'I don't remember that!' He turned back to Turlough. 'Find the TARDIS and stay with Tegan and Nyssa. Brigadier, I want you to come with me.' He hurried the older man into the narrow side-passage, leaving Turlough alone again on the alien ship.

Turlough hoped that the Doctor was not walking into a trap. . . But that was ridiculous. *The Doctor must be destroyed.* Yet without the Doctor's help, how could he ever free the ship from the warp ellipse? He felt very confused.

He reached for the cube. Since his purpose was now evil, his guide must be the Black Guardian. As he held the crystal he cringed at his own weakness and inadequacy in the service of his new master. 'It's not my fault the Doctor was able to home in on the TARDIS,' he pleaded.

The crystal was lifeless in his hand.

'Can you hear me?'

There was no stinging rebuke or diabolical resassurance.

'There's not much I can do with the Brigadier around. . . Answer me!' he cried.

But there was no answer. Rejected and afraid, Turlough moved into the darkness.

A bulkhead sealed the end of the side passage. 'A dead end,' thought the Brigadier. But the Doctor was already fingering the ornamentation around the edge of the door. There was a click and the door slid sideways.

The room they entered was unlike anywhere else in the ship; functional, unembellished, cold as a mortuary.

'Some kind of a laboratory,' muttered the Brigadier. 'Or could it be an operating theatre?' He could make nothing of the sinister machinery.

Not so the Doctor. 'A metamorphic symbiosis regenerator!' He moved excitedly to a large piece of apparatus in the centre of the room.

The Brigadier thought longingly of the safe, comfortable technology of his old Humber; but he was far from the world of vintage cars and A-level maths.

'Used by the Time Lords in cases of acute regenerative crisis,' continued the Doctor after a cursory examination of the machine.

'Then what's it doing there?'

The same question was worrying the Doctor. 'It must have been stolen from Gallifrey!' He turned, grim-faced, to the Brigadier. 'Someone on this ship has been trying to regenerate.'

'The injured creature that Tegan thought was you?'

The Doctor leaned over the regenerator. 'This would explain the mutation.'

'Where is he now?' The Brigadier looked anxiously out into the empty passage. 'Perhaps he didn't make it in time. Collapsed somewhere. Even dead?'

'Or *undead*, Brigadier!'

In the course of his military career the Brigadier

had faced danger many times, but as he pictured that deformed creature at large on the ship – a potential enemy that could never be killed – his blood ran cold. He thought once again of the legend of the Flying Dutchman.

'Look at this, Brigadier!' The Doctor indicated several pieces of trunking, each terminating in a frame mounted with a complicated set of electrodes, that connected with the metamorphosis machine. 'Eight of them!' he whispered ominously.

The old soldier was none the wiser.

'Somewhere on this ship, Brigadier, there are seven more creatures!'

Turlough could never explain what had prompted him to linger in the Hall of the Likenesses. He stood in the side gallery, mesmerised by the bland faces. As he moved a step forward, he could have sworn the eyes of the central icon blinked. He gazed at the portrait. . . And back at Turlough stared the Black Guardian. Turlough gasped at the sudden transformation.

'While the Doctor is alive, I am never far from you, Turlough.'

'I'm sorry. I wasn't to know the Doctor had a homing device.' He began to tremble.

'Whimpering boy! Do you not understand! Everything now works towards the total humiliation of the Time Lord.' The Black Guardian smiled. 'You have done well.'

Turlough tried to stop himself shaking.

'Give me your hand.'

The boy would as willingly have offered his arm to a hooded cobra.

'Give me your hand. There is nothing to fear.'

82

The Black Guardian vanished the moment his fingers touched the likeness, and the whole frame swung back to reveal a hidden room. Turlough stepped into the chamber.

It felt as though he had entered a charnel-house. As his eyes grew accustomed to the light he became aware of seven shadowy figures, like corpses in their winding sheets, laid out against the walls. He peered at the sepulchral shapes; each shroud he saw to be a set of rich clothes, as sumptuous as the fabric of the ship itself. Each of the robes, he supposed, must enclose a dead man. But why had the Black Guardian sent him to open up a tomb?

There was a soft wheezing, as if an old man had began to snore. It came again; and again. Turlough realised that each cadaverous occupant of the chamber was struggling to draw air into his lungs; somehow the opening of the door had brought the creatures to life. He was paralysed with fear.

The hooded things began to stir. Bodies flexed under velvet cloaks; twisted arms started to tear off their sheaths and flail in the empty air around the terrified boy. The creature nearest Turlough lifted a claw-like hand and tore the cloth from his face. For a full five seconds, Turlough faced the hideous, gasping mutant, then screamed, and fled.

The resurrected corpse that had sent Turlough scuttling away down the corridor focused its sunken eyes on the open door. 'Mawdryn has returned,' it announced to its fellow sleepers.

'Does he bring hope of our ending?' came the reply.

The Brigadier couldn't wait to get out of the laboratory. There was something very disturbing about all those sterile, white panels with their inset dials and switches, and those tortuous electrodes.

But the Doctor was still examining the regenerator. 'There've been some very cunning modifications. . .' A vicious buzzing emanated from the centre of the machine as the Doctor moved one of the switches.

'That all looks highly dangerous,' warned the Brigadier.

'Quite right,' agreed the Doctor. 'It could do very nasty things to a genuine Time Lord.'

'Listen!' The Brigadier had heard the sound of a voice in the corridor. Or was it only the echo of the machinery the Doctor had set in motion? He moved quietly into the connecting passage to investigate, leaving the Doctor alone with the regenerator.

'Doctor? Doctor?' A younger, sprucer Lethbridge-Stewart advanced slowly along the main companionway. He was fairly confident, now, that the wounded man he was searching for was an imposter, but it would do no harm to give him the benefit of a little more doubt. 'Doctor!' he called again, pausing beside the small passage to the laboratory.

It was odd for someone as observant as Brigadier Lethbridge-Stewart not to notice the narrow entrance, but he was distracted by the increase in static electricity; the tingling on the back of his neck had returned.

Mawdryn moved silently as he writhed and wriggled towards the laboratory. As soon as he regained consciousness he had sensed the presence of more outsiders. Perhaps the Time Lord had come in search of his TARDIS.

Without the help of his fellow mutants, his progress

was desperately slow, but he was not far now from the regenerator.

Had Mawdryn arrived a moment sooner at the approach to the laboratory, he would have been amazed to see *two* Brigadiers: one dressed in military blazer and tie who stood massaging his neck; the other a fatter, older man in a tweed jacket who appeared from the direction of the lab, a split second too late to catch sight of his other self at the junction, as the younger Lethbridge-Stewart moved off along the main corridor.

The senior Brigadier scratched his wrists which had begun to tingle again. He stepped forward and looked up and down the main companionway. The old soldier was sure someone was calling, further along the corridor. He followed the sound.

'Are you there, Brigadier?' The Doctor hurried from the narrow side-passage and peered into the corridor. How annoying of old Lethbridge-Stewart to wander off. He must have gone ahead to look for the TARDIS. The Doctor checked his bearings; the police box must be somewhere down there. . .

As Mawdryn squirmed forward he sensed the aura of the Time Lord whom he could dimly see hurrying away down the corridor. He dragged himself, like a slug, into the side passage and towards the laboratory.

One of the memories that had come flooding back to the old Brigadier was that UNIT's former scientific advisor should not be trusted on his own. Lethbridge-Stewart was therefore reluctant to leave the Doctor tinkering with that diabolical machine, and since there was no way he could follow the mystery voice without getting hopelessly lost, he retraced his steps to the laboratory.

'Doctor, we must move on!'

The regenerator was humming even more ferociously than before, but there was no sign of the Doctor.

'Now where's he gone?'

'Brigadier!'

The Brigadier was on the point of leaving when he heard the guttural whisper from the floor behind the machine. He took a step forward. There was another croak, and he looked down.

'Help me, Brigadier!'

The Brigadier's stomach heaved. He had never seen so mutilated and deformed a face that was part of a living creature. But he had seen the coat before, stained though it was with gore and suppuration. It belonged to the Doctor.

6

Rising of the Undead

Tegan and Nyssa were bored with waiting in the
TARDIS.

'I'm going after the Brigadier,' decided Tegan.

'But he told us to stay here.'

'We're not in the Army!'

'You could get lost.'

'Stay here if you want to. I want to find the Doctor.
The real Doctor.'

'Does this one qualify?'

The two girls spun round, amazed and delighted at
the familiar figure in the doorway.

'Where's Turlough?' asked the Doctor, who had
expected to find him already in the TARDIS.

'You brought that boy with you?'

'And the Brigadier, but it seems I've lost both of
them.'

'How could the Brigadier have been with you. He
came with us?'

The Doctor looked at Tegan, unable to believe what
he had just heard. 'How could you be so stupid!' he
shouted.

The worst had happened. Two Lethbridge-Stewarts,
the same man but drawn concurrently from 1977 and

1983, were both at large on the ship. At any moment they risked the appalling and unpredictable consequences of the Blinovitch Limitation Effect.

'Come on! We've got to find them!' cried the Doctor, rushing from the control room.

Turlough ran, panic-stricken, down one long corridor after another, terrified that the creatures he had disturbed in the hidden chamber were after him.

He stopped. There at the bottom of the staircase was the Doctor's police box. Safety at last.

The control room was empty – the perfect opportunity. He would steal the TARDIS.

He poured over the console. With a little experimentation he could surely make the thing work.

'You will not be able to operate the TARDIS!'

The Black Guardian glowered from the scanner screen.

'I can work it if you show me how!' shouted Turlough defiantly. 'Then the Doctor will be trapped and I can escape. Isn't that the agreement?'

'Do you think I have controlled you merely to prick the flesh of this presumtuous Gallifreyan?'

Turlough was near despair. 'What more do you want of me!' he pleaded.

'The friend of the Doctor's is at present on the ship in two aspects. You must find the Brigadier who travelled with the Doctor's companions.'

Turlough slumped despondently over the console. But his evil master would condone no weakness. 'The co-existence of the Earthling is hazardous to our plans. The two Brigadiers must be kept apart.'

'But those creatures!' protested Turlough, thinking of the living corpses that by now must roam the ship.

'The mutants released from the dormition chamber threaten only the Time Lord!'

Suddenly, Turlough understood that the ship, the undead things from the chamber, the Brigadier, his own sabotage of the transmitter were mere elements of a master plan, the climax of a cosmic vendetta. With the Doctor destroyed, the bargain he had made, indeed his own life, would be worth nothing.

He gave a quick glance at the dematerialisation control. Perhaps he could spiral the TARDIS out into time/space, and free himself from the evil. . .

'Turlough!'

Even as the thought of escape came into the boy's mind he felt the pain in his forehead and the voice of the Black Guardian reverberated inside his skull. 'You will remain on the ship and witness the nemesis of the Doctor!'

It had not been a pleasant task dragging the cankered body up from the floor of the Laboratory, but the Brigadier was far too worried about the Doctor to feel squeamish. If only his old friend had kept his hands off that machine.

Following the instructions that issued from the shrunken head, the Brigadier positioned the decomposing body in one of the frames that connected with the regenerator. He obediently positioned the electrodes and, albeit reluctantly, switched on the apparatus.

The speed of the healing process astounded him.

'The energy repairs the depredation of the transmat capsule.' The Doctor sounded stronger already.

The Doctor? Brigadier Lethbridge-Stewart peered at the alien face reforming between the electrodes. 'You're not the Doctor at all!'

'I am Mawdryn.'

The Brigadier was angry at being fooled into helping the enemy. 'Where is the Doctor?' he shouted.

'I do not know.'

'You're lying.'

Mawdryn shook his head.

'Unless you tell me I shall turn off your life-support system.'

Mawdryn smiled sadly. 'It does not matter.'

'I imagine it matters to you if you die!' The Brigadier moved his hand to the controls of the regenerator.

Mawdryn stared at the Brigadier with such a look of pain and longing. For a moment the old soldier's mind went back thirty-five years to his first taste of action as a young lieutenant in Palestine, with his platoon badly shot up by terrorists, and he remembered the mangled conscript who screamed at the officer to take his rifle and kill him.

Mawdryn groaned. 'Without the energy only our shape will change.' He gave a deep sigh. 'Our endless voyage will never cease. We cannot die.'

The younger Brigadier moved cautiously through the ship. As he paused at the junction of two corridors, there was a distant rustling which sent him darting into the shadows. Round the corner came seven figures in wide flowing cloaks, which glided past within inches of where Lethbridge-Stewart was pressed up against the wall. He recoiled in horror as he glimpsed their terrible cowled faces.

'Stay here,' said the Doctor to Tegan as they reached the narrow turning to the laboratory. If *your* Brigadier comes past, stop him.' Followed by Nyssa, he made his way up the passage and into the laboratory.

Both the Doctor and the Brigadier were delighted to see each other. 'Thank goodness you're all right!' cried the Doctor, who had never expected to track down the older Lethbridge-Stewart so easily. With one half of the duo under control they could avoid the Blinovitch Limitation Effect.

'Doctor! Over there!' screamed Nyssa, pointing at Mawdryn, who was still drawing energy from the regenerator. 'That's *him*!'

With a sense of deep foreboding the Doctor walked over to the master of the ghostly vessel. The alien smiled coldly. 'I am Mawdryn. Welcome to my ship, Time Lord.'

'So it was you who stole the regenerator from Gallifrey.'

'Yes, Doctor. But time itself has punished us for the crime.'

'You modified that machine?' The Doctor looked at Mawdryn in awe. 'You created endless life for yourselves?'

'Endless torment!' Mawdryn's face twisted with physical and mental distress. 'Our bodies eternally renewed in a vile travesty of our former selves.'

The Doctor was appalled. 'You induced a perpetual mutation?' he whispered.

'So horrible,' replied Mawdryn bitterly, 'that we were exiled in this ship.'

'How were you able to come to Earth?'

'It is decreed; every seventy years, the beacons guide the ship to within transmat distance of a planet. While seven of our company sleep, one of us may leave the ship to seek help.'

But the Doctor knew, as well as Mawdryn, that there was no help; the red ship was destined to orbit eternally with its crew of mutants, their bodies spared from inexorable degeneration only by the power of the regenerator. But whether they continued to live in the luxurious and stabilising confines of the ship, or floated amoeba-like in the void of space, they would never die.

'It is the Time Lords' curse!'

'The curse of your own criminal ambition,' answered the Doctor, sternly.

'The Time Lords could have helped us, but we were abandoned.'

'Time Lords cannot become involved.' The Doctor spoke as if the law was inviolate, yet it was a rule he had broken many times.

Mawdryn said nothing.

The Doctor turned away, unable to meet the mutant's gaze. He was trembling. Was this, he wondered, the ultimate coincidence? Had he been hounded, through time and space, in despite of infinite improbability, to this fateful confrontation?

'Doctor!' There was a shriek from the corridor and Tegan came running in. She had spotted the seven mutants from the dormition chamber making their way to the laboratory.

'My brothers in exile,' explained Mawdryn, scornful of the Earthchild's fear. 'They need the regenerator.'

Tegan turned spitefully to Mawdryn. 'I always knew you weren't the Doctor!'

'Look out!' shouted the Brigadier, as, one by one, the seven undead, released unwittingly by Turlough from the chamber, entered the laboratory.

The seven years of sleeping had been a blessed respite from their torment, but it had taken a heavy toll of their substance. As if shamed by the presence of uncontaminated mortals, they gathered their cloaks

92

over their rotting features, as, one by one, they joined themselves to the stolen machine.

'Who are they?' whispered Brigadier Lethbridge-Stewart.

'Scientists who tried to turn themselves into Time Lords,' said the Doctor. 'But it all went horribly wrong.'

'It is eternal agony!' cried Mawdryn. 'That is why we long for the ending.'

'These people. . .' Tegan stared, horrified, at the gasping mutants. 'They're immortal?'

'Yes. For what it's worth.'

The regenerator hummed noisily. Each mutant was growing stronger. The Doctor backed nervously away to the door.

'Doctor!' Mawdryn called. 'The life-force flows. Join yourself with us.'

'No!' shouted the Doctor.

'Give us the life-force from a Time Lord,' pleaded the leader. 'The abberation will resolve and our suffering will end.'

'Never!'

The Brigadier, Tegan and Nyssa were amazed to see the Doctor so afraid.

'For pity's sake,' begged the mutant. 'You cannot refuse.'

The Doctor turned his back on Mawdryn and his seven companions.

Even Tegan was upset by such coldness. 'Why can't you help them, Doctor?'

The Doctor rounded angrily on his companion. 'A Time Lord can only regenerate twelve times. I have already done so four times.'

'So?'

'Don't you see!' shouted the Doctor, desperate to

escape from the laboratory. 'Eight of them. Eight of me!'

The silent eyes of the eight mutants never left the Time Lord. The Doctor felt paralysed by their desperate need.

'They want my eight remaining lives to end their mutation,' he whispered, white with anxiety. 'They want to take away my own regenerative powers!'

7

Double Danger of the Brigadier

Turlough searched nervously for the Brigadier who had come with Tegan and Nyssa from 1977. He was not convinced that the sleepers from the dormition chamber were as harmless as the Black Guardian claimed, and was anxious to avoid a second confrontation.

He darted behind a convenient piece of abstract sculpture. Someone – or something – was coming towards him. Turlough smiled as he spotted the dapper blazered figure walking slowly down the corridor. It was the Brigadier, all right; but this confident, strutting, military man was not the Brigadier that Turlough knew. What was more to the point, neither did this – the younger Brigadier – as yet know Turlough.

'Hello, Brigadier!' Turlough stepped out in front of a startled Lethbridge-Stewart.

'Who the devil are you?'

'Turlough, of course,' said Turlough mischievously.

'Heard about you from Tegan,' said his future maths master.

So this, thought the Brigadier to himself, was the famous Turlough. Just wait till the boy got to Brendon. He'd have that impudent grin off his face.

'I've come to take you to the Doctor,' continued Turlough insolently.

'The Doctor? You know where he is?'

'Of course. Come on.'

'Not so fast,' growled the Brigadier. 'And keep in the shadows. We've got some disagreeable fellow passengers.'

Turlough was far more afraid of the mutants than the Brigadier, but he was keen to score off the military man in the blazer. 'They're harmless,' he jeered. 'You're not afraid, are you?'

The Brigadier could have boxed his future pupil's ears for cheek, but he said nothing and followed the boy in the direction of the Hall of Likenesses. 'What does this Doctor look like?' he asked as they walked past the icons.

'Older than me. Younger than you.'

'I mean, is he . . . normal?'

'Of course.'

'Then that deformed creature in the TARDIS was an imposter!'

Turlough stopped at the open door of the dormition chamber. 'Doctor? The Brigadier's here.'

The Brigadier peered over Turlough's shoulder. He pushed the boy aside and stepped into the inner room. 'Doctor?' He wrinkled his nose at the faintly rank odour, akin to overipe pheasant, that hung about the chamber. 'Doctor?'

There was a rumble and a click. The Brigadier spun round to see the entrance behind him sealed. The wretched boy had led him into a trap.

'We are scientists,' explained the mutant leader to the Brigadier as he tried to hurry the Doctor to the safety of his TARDIS. 'The Doctor can help us only of his own free will.'

'You cannot ask me to change my whole nature,' the Doctor repeated stonily as Mawdryn pleaded with him to end their infinite journey.

'Come on, Doctor, we're getting out of here,' whispered Tegan.

But still the Doctor lingered by the regenerator. He could not believe he was destined to escape so easily. 'You have the regenerator and the facilities of the laboratory. Continue with your experiments. Find how to reverse the process.'

'We have known for many years that the process is irreversible.'

Nyssa moved to the Doctor's side. 'There must be something you can do to help them.'

'Don't interfere!' The Doctor silenced her angrily. 'I cannot will my own destruction.'

'So be it,' said Mawdryn wearily. 'Leave now with the rest of your companions. But accept the consequences of your own actions.'

The other mutants began to murmur in protest. 'Go quickly,' urged Mawdryn.

'That sounds like good advice.' The Brigadier grabbed the Doctor by the arm and propelled him towards the door.

'We have experimented for centuries,' clamoured the mutant lying next to Mawdryn.

'We have tried to discover a remedy,' cried his companion.

'There is no remission,' moaned another in despair.

'Only the power in you, Time Lord!'

'Only you can help us, Doctor. Share the life-force with us, that we may grow old and die!'

The Doctor stood watching them like a sailor who

has seen his shipmate fall overboard, and knows that, while the boat sails on, the castaway must surely die.

'Come on, Doctor,' urged Tegan. 'There's nothing that any of us can do.'

The Doctor turned reluctantly to go. Filled with dismay, the mutants struggled to free themselves from the regenerator.

'To the TARDIS, the lot of you!' roared the Brigadier and shepherded the Doctor, Tegan and Nyssa out into the corridor.

The mutants howled like abandoned children and would have rushed into the passageway to drag the Doctor back into the laboratory had they been strong enough.

'My friends, do not despair,' Mawdryn comforted his fellow exiles. 'The Doctor will return, and of his own free will.' He detached himself from the machine and stood, tall and strong, as any normal creature. Only the ulcerous sarcoma on the right of his face branded him as unnatural. 'There is work to be done,' he announced gravely. His seven comrades looked at him, hardly daring to hope. Then he spoke the words they had waited over two thousand years to hear. 'Prepare our ship for the ending!'

As they rushed along the sombre corridors towards the TARDIS, Tegan noticed how out of breath the Brigadier was getting. The poor man had certainly gone to pieces in those six years since she was at Brendon School – put on weight too, she observed, as he paused to get his breath back. 'I'm Tegan by the way,' she said, introducing herself with a friendly smile. 'We have met, but it was rather a long time ago.'

'Miss Jovanka, could I ever forget,' puffed the breathless Sir Galahad of Jubilee Day.

'Doctor, what are we going to do about Turlough?' asked Nyssa.

'Turlough will have found the TARDIS by now.'

'And the other Brigadier?'

'I can only deal with one Brigadier at a time!' snapped the Doctor, desperate to reach the police box and get clear of the alien ship.

'What's that?' Lethbridge-Stewart pricked up his ears.

The Doctor explained to the horrified old soldier the presence of his six years' junior on board Mawdryn's ship. The senior Brigadier was none too happy about the way the Doctor proposed to leave part of him adrift in space.

'You were perfectly all right in 1983,' the Doctor explained impatiently. 'Obviously your 1977 persona came to no harm.'

The Brigadier, who by now didn't know whether he was coming or going, entered the TARDIS with the two girls, still grumbling about spending six years in limbo.

'No sign of Turlough,' said Tegan, looking round the control room.'

'Never trusted that boy,' muttered the Brigadier testily.

'Maybe he's exploring the TARDIS?'

'I hope so,' said the Doctor, already setting a course out of the warp ellipse, 'because we've got to get the TARDIS away from here.'

'Look!' Nyssa pointed to the scanner.

Running down the corridor, terrified that the TARDIS was leaving without him, was Turlough.

Turlough had felt rather pleased with himself at trapping the younger Brigadier so neatly inside the dormition chamber. That would settle a few scores with the cantankerous old pedagogue – albeit prospectively. He grinned at the paradox: the prisoner from 1977 was, as yet, a stranger.

There were no congratulations, however, from the Black Guardian; no voice; no glowing presence. He took out the cube – a mere piece of glass.

Turlough strolled along the marble ambulatories, exploring libraries and galleries, luxurious salons and halls of recreation.

He began to feel lonely. Perhaps the Doctor was already dead; and the girls; and the older Brigadier. He had been abandoned!

He was on the point of returning to open up the dormition chamber – if only for the doubtful company of the junior Brigadier – when he heard the voices.

From behind a gilded buttress, he could see the Doctor and his companions, alive and well and on their way back to the TARDIS. Could the Doctor be escaping? Had the Black Guardian failed? Turlough followed at a distance, and saw the Doctor, the girls and the senior Brigadier all disappear into the police box.

It suddenly occurred to the boy that, with the TARDIS gone and the Black Guardian, maybe, defeated, he would be marooned on the ship. He rushed panic-stricken towards the time-machine.

To Turlough's surprise, the Doctor met him in the doorway.

'Turlough, listen very carefully.' An unusually agitated Doctor explained the problem of the two Brigadiers.

As if it were one of Canon Whitstable's anecdotes, Turlough pretended he was hearing it all for the first time.

'Find the Brigadier and take him to the transmat capsule,' ordered the Doctor.

'But the transmat beam doesn't work.'

'The capsule is locked in to the TARDIS homing device. When you operate the capsule it will transmat to the centre of the TARDIS.'

Turlough nodded.

'When you arrive in the TARDIS, stay in the capsule. Don't let the Brigadier out until I tell you it's safe.' The Doctor slammed the door. The light on the police box flashed, there was a grinding sound – and a rather bemused Turlough was alone in the corridor.

The Doctor was delighted to have escaped from the red ship so easily. 'It takes a very cunning setting of the co-ordinates to clear a warp ellipse,' he boasted from beside the console.

The two girls were more subdued. 'Will the mutants really travel for the rest of time?' asked Nyssa.

For some reason the Doctor would not look either of them in the face. 'Sometimes you have to live with the consequences of your actions,' he replied coldly.

'That's terrible.' Nyssa was close to tears; but the Doctor pretended not to notice.

'Doctor!' shouted Tegan suddenly.

'Something's happening,' Nyssa gasped.

'Not at all,' replied the Doctor, still concentrating on his navigation. 'We're on course for Brendon School in 1983.'

'Doctor!' The Brigadier, who had been watching the two girls for several moments, cried out in horror. The Doctor spun round. Nothing could have prepared him for the appalling sight of his two companions.

Tegan's auburn hair had turned white. Wrinkles raced across her face like cracks in thin ice, and her teeth were beginning to leer from shrunken gums; she was suddenly as old as the hills.

Nyssa's skin, too, was a network of puckering pleats and lines, her mouth gaunt and twisted as a crone's.

'What's happening!' shouted the Brigadier.

The Doctor just stared, amazed beyond belief, at the time-worn faces of the girls.

'Doctor, do something!' cackled the senile Nyssa.

'Please . . . Doctor!' Hardly more than a death rattle came from Tegan's throat.

'Tegan . . . Nyssa . . .' stammered the Doctor helplessly.

The young girls's clothes hung limply round the bodies of the shrinking hags. Older and older grew the two companions as the TARDIS travelled through time and space. Soon their flesh would be dust.

'Like Mawdryn in the lab,' whispered the Brigadier, peering aghast at Tegan and Nyssa's withering bodies.

'Mawdryn!' cried the Doctor. 'They've been contaminated. . .' He had only the merest intuition of the terrible syndrome from which, within minutes, both girls would surely be dead. He wracked his brains for some quick antidote. 'The transfiguration can be contained,' he muttered, desperately near panic.

'Stop!' Nyssa's strangled cry was barely audible, but the Doctor immediately leaped to the console.

'Stop! That's it!' He instantly reversed the co-ordinates. 'Travelling through time has accelerated the degeneration.'

The Brigadier looked over the Doctor's shoulder at the flashing lights on the console. 'You've stopped the TARDIS?'

'More than that.' The Doctor stared anxiously at the mummified faces of Tegan and Nyssa. 'We're going

102

back to where we started. I just hope it induces a proportional remission.'

The younger Brigadier's knuckles were raw with banging against the walls of his prison. He had explored every inch of the sealed chamber and attacked the surround of the door with penknife, pipe-cleaners and ballpoint pen, but to no avail. If ever he caught up with that impudent whippersnapper, Turlough. . .

He found himself staring at the ornamentation around the door. Part of the frieze seemed to be loose. He ran his hand gently over the entablature; there was a click, and the door swung back. He was free.

Weak with relief the Doctor knelt over the two exhausted girls.

'It worked!' observed the Brigadier gruffly, equally gratified to see Tegan and Nyssa returned to their normal selves.

'Doctor, what went wrong?'

The Doctor tried to describe the infection they must have picked up when they carried Mawdryn into the TARDIS; a viral side-effect of the mutants' constant experimentation. The Brigadier wondered, ominously, whether he too would succumb to his brief contact with the creature in the laboratory.

'So we can't travel through time?' said Nyssa, as she realised the implications of what the Doctor had just told them.

'We don't need to time-travel,' interrupted Tegan, who only wanted to get back to Earth.

The Doctor shook his head. 'I have to programme a temporal deviation to escape the warp ellipse.'

'Look!' The Brigadier pointed at the scanner.

Standing, like a guard of honour, outside the

TARDIS, dressed in their finest robes, were Mawdryn and his brothers in exile.

'They knew this was going to happen.'

'That's why they let us go so easily,' said the Doctor bitterly.

'You mean we're stuck on this ship?'

'I wonder!' The Doctor returned defiantly to the console. 'If I reversed the trajectory. . .'

'The Doctor will not give up so easily,' said Mawdryn to his comrades, as the TARDIS dematerialised a second time. The confident smile disappeared from his face as a middle-aged Earthman in a blue blazer rushed into the empty space left by the police box.

It had never occured to the younger Lethbridge-Stewart, when he left to reconnoitre the ship, that the time-machine could leave without him, and it had been a considerable shock as he turned the corner by the staircase, to see the light on the police box already flashing. He sprinted forward . . . but too late.

The presence of the alien from the TARDIS, together with seven more of similar ilk was a further surprise to the Brigadier. But it was nothing to the confusion and dismay of the eight vigilants at his own arrival.

'Brigadier!' exclaimed Mawdryn, who had just seen the same military gentleman leave with the Doctor.

'This man is also in the TARDIS,' warned a fellow Mutant.

'He is a deviant!' cried another.

'There has been temporal duplication!'

There was consternation amongst the mutants.

'The TARDIS will soon return. The imbalance could be cataclysmic,' declared Mawdryn. 'For your own safety you must return to Earth at once.' He grabbed the Brigadier by the arm and hurried him in the direction of the control centre.

'So far so good.' The older version of Brigadier Lethbridge-Stewart was anxiously watching Tegan and Nyssa as they time-travelled away from the ship. The Doctor stood beside the console, hand poised over the controls.

'It's no good!' wailed Nyssa in a plaintive voice.

'But nothing's happening,' protested the Brigadier.

'Oh yes it is,' said the Doctor in despair.

Lethbridge-Stewart looked more closely at the two girls. There was a look of bland innocence on Nyssa's face, a softening of the aggressive line of Tegan's jaw. They were both suddenly thinner, shorter. . .

'We're travelling in the opposite direction,' explained the Doctor. 'It's having the reverse effect.'

'Stop! Stop!' piped the voices of two tiny children.

As Tegan and Nyssa regressed towards infancy, the Doctor reversed the direction of the TARDIS.

Mawdryn returned from the control centre in time to see the police box rematerialise at the foot of the stairs. Everything was happening as he had predicted. All things proceeded towards the ending.

Leaving the Brigadier to comfort his two companions, the Doctor returned to the console where an intermittent buzzing had begun to sound in the communications section. Someone must be trying to operate the transmat capsule. 'Obviously Turlough taking your other half to the centre of the TARDIS.' He explained his plan for avoiding the Blinovitch Limitation Effect to the older Brigadier.

'Can the capsule do that?'

'Only when the TARDIS is clear of the ship. Until that happens the transmat can't take place. The capsule will return to its terminal.'

The junior Brigadier opened the door of the silver sphere into which he had been so unceremoniously bundled. He was still on board the alien's ship. Lethbridge-Stewart was not surprised; he had never really believed the creature when he pretended to be the Doctor, and he certainly wasn't going to be persuaded that this bauble would transmit him to Earth.

There was a sudden bleeping, quite different from the whirring and buzzing when he operated the so-called transmat control. He caught sight of a rather familiar round object wired into the control panel. He could swear that was the Doctor's homing device. But how. . . As the Brigadier's hand went to his blazer pocket, it froze as if paralysed by an electric shock – that deuced static again.

He looked at the globe in front of him and smiled. That was the homing device all right – indicating the presence of the TARDIS. The alien could keep his transmat capsule. This one was going home by police box.

Turlough returned reluctantly to the dormition chamber. He had no reason to believe that the younger Brigadier would prove any less blisteringly choleric at his incarceration than would have been the older, and more familiar schoolmaster. But he needed to follow the Doctor's instructions, if only to guarantee his escape from the ship. At least, with the 1983 Lethbridge-Stewart safely on his way back to Earth, the release of the prisoner behind the icon could hardly upset the Black Guardian. Not that he particularly cared; the owner of the TARDIS would appear to have got the better of the man in black.

As he approached the inner door he saw the open door. An ominous red glow filled the chamber. Turlough began to shiver.

'You have failed me!' The voice of the Black Guardian reverberated angrily in the empty room.

'No!' Turlough trembled in the doorway.

'The Brigadier is free.'

'I'm sorry.'

'So near the annihilation of the Doctor, and you risk all with your negligence and stupidity.'

So the Doctor had not escaped from the ship at all. 'I can still keep the two Lethbridge-Stewarts apart,' pleaded the boy.

When the unseen voice sounded again, it was darker and more terrible than ever before. 'If you fail me again, I shall destroy you, Turlough!'

The Doctor leaned despondently over the console. There was nothing he could do to clear the ship without hurting the two girls.

'What are we going to do?' asked Nyssa.

The Doctor was silent.

'We can't stay in the TARDIS for ever.'

They all looked up at the scanner with its view of the reception committee outside.

'Well, Doctor?' said the Brigadier.

Still without saying a word, the Doctor opened the main doors and walked out of the control room.

The Time Lord stood aloof from the rest of them, his head slightly bowed. It was Nyssa who confronted Mawdryn. 'You knew that would happen!'

'Yes, Nyssa.' Mawdryn spoke with unexpected tenderness. 'But there was no conspiracy to harm you.'

'What happens now?' asked Tegan.

'You will remain on the ship.'

Tegan was stunned. 'For the rest of our lives?'

'You are fortunate,' said Mawdryn sadly. 'Your journey will be short. Ours is without end.'

Nyssa and Tegan looked disbelievingly at each other, then turned to the Doctor.

The Doctor said nothing.

Brigadier Lethbridge-Stewart took a step towards the mutants. 'We are not leaving those two girls on your ship.'

'Take them with you in the TARDIS,' replied Mawdryn, 'and they will die.'

'Are you telling me that with all those facilities you can't come up with some sort of antidote?'

'We have no restorative for Tegan and Nyssa.'

'Doctor, you must have some ideas?'

The Doctor said nothing.

Lethbridge-Stewart turned back to Mawdryn. 'When we were in the laboratory you claimed the Doctor could help you through that machinery.'

'Yes, but only of his own free will.'

'Then he can do the same for Tegan and Nyssa?'

'That is a question you must ask the Doctor.'

'Well, Doctor?' said the Brigadier.

The Doctor said nothing.

The eight mutants stared at the Time Lord.

'Doctor!' pleaded Tegan.

'Doctor!' begged Nyssa.

'Take me to your laboratory,' said the Doctor to Mawdryn.

The procession advanced slowly along the corridor.

First, seven mutants in their finery; then Mawdryn and the Brigadier – an odd partner in his hacking jacket and cavalry twills; then the girls; and finally the Doctor, proud and silent, like a condemned man determined to die with dignity.

Mawdryn spoke the Doctor's epitaph as he walked with Brigadier Lethbridge-Stewart. 'The Doctor is a Time Lord, but he chose to involve himself; soon he will be a Time Lord no longer. That is his reward for compassion.'

Just as he had thought – the TARDIS had come back to the ship! The Brigadier from 1977 hurried into the control room. It was deserted. What were those two young women up to now!

Turlough had seen the procession enter the laboratory. That was one Brigadier accounted for. Now he had only to track down the younger Lethbridge-Stewart.

'Doctor!'

Turlough held his breath.

'Doctor? Tegan? Nyssa?'

The voice came from a nearby corridor. Turlough crept towards his quarry.

All eight mutants were once more connected to the regenerator. So, too, were the Doctor, Nyssa and Tegan.

'*You* will activate the energy transfer, Brigadier,' instructed Mawdryn. 'It will take several seconds for the charge in the machine to build up. You will read off the countdown to the moment of exchange.'

Brigadier Lethbridge-Stewart nodded grimly. Tegan and Nyssa glanced nervously at each other.

'Do not be afraid,' said the mutant wired up beside

them. 'When the moment comes we will *all* share in the life-force of the Doctor.'

'Our mutation will end,' said another, his eyes shining with expectation.'

'And *you* will no longer be contaminated.'

'And the Doctor won't be a Time Lord any more,' said Nyssa guiltily.

The Doctor, electrodes festooned round his head, stared stoically ahead.

'My brothers in exile.' Mawdryn's voice shook with emotion. 'We approach the ending!' He pointed to the master control. 'Activate, Brigadier!'

There was a low whine as the power began to surge within the regenerator.

'Twenty seconds,' announced Brigadier Lethbridge-Stewart.

'Brigadier!' shouted Turlough, running wildly down the corridor. Somehow he had missed the other man. He felt the fury of the Black Guardian possess him.

'So near the supreme moment!' The voice, thundering in his brain, seemed to vibrate the whole ship. 'The Brigadiers must not converge. Find him! Find the Brigadier at once!'

The younger Brigadier was intrigued by the strange sound coming from the narrow side-passage.

'Brigadier!'

Someone was racing towards him down the main corridor. Turlough again! He would deal with that young man later. For the moment, there was something very strange going on in the brightly lit room at the end of the passageway.

'Ten, nine, eight. . .'

He could hear a voice, curiously familiar, but difficult to place.

'Brigadier!' Turlough had almost caught up.

'Stop him!' howled the Black Guardian, 'or I shall destroy you all!'

'Seven six. . .'

'Brigadier, come back!' Turlough grabbed the arm of the man in the blazer, but was pushed roughly aside.

The Brigadier from 1977 entered the laboratory.

'Five, four. . .' The Brigadier from 1983 read off the final countdown.

The intruder was momentarily hypnotised by the spectacle of eight mutants, conjoined in a ganglion of tubes and wires. Then he caught sight of a young man in a frock-coat, also connected to the apparatus. 'What the devil. . . !'

'Three. . .'

The newcomer took a step forward, and, to his disgust and horror, saw Tegan and Nyssa lashed to the same devilish torture machine.

'Two. . .'

'Brigadier, get out of here!' yelled the young man.

The Brigadier took no notice, but advanced towards the swine at the controls.

'One second. . .'

'What do you think you're doing!'

The operator turned.

For a moment time stood still. Brigadier stared at Brigadier, then, as their hands touched, there was a blinding flash and a tremendous explosion.

111

8

All Present and Correct

Turlough ran and ran and ran, as if perpetual movement would keep the vengeance of the Black Guardian from him.

He finally stopped from sheer exhaustion, feeling strangely light-headed. He took out the cube; it was cracked. Was this all part of the Blinovitch Limitation Effect? Could he even be . . . free?

Turlough set off, purposefully, in the direction of the TARDIS.

Tegan and Nyssa regained consciousness as the smoke was clearing in the laboratory. They opened their eyes to see the Doctor unwiring them from the regenerator.

'What happened?' murmured Tegan.

'An immense discharge of energy as the two Brigadiers came together, exactly synchronising with the moment of transfer.' The Doctor walked over to examine the body of a man in a blue blazer, lying beside the regenerator.

'Is the Brigadier dead?'

'No,' said the Doctor, in the certain knowledge that the unconscious Lethbridge-Stewart had at least another six years of life ahead of him.

'Doctor!' Nyssa had spotted the prone figure of another, older Brigadier, with a totally uncertain future, who lay in his singed sports jacket, on the far side of the laboratory.

The Doctor rushed across and knelt beside the old soldier, feeling anxiously for his pulse. For an agonising moment, he felt nothing. The Doctor groaned. That he should have caused the death of his oldest, most trusted ally on the planet Earth, was unendurable.

Then he felt the faint but steady beat as the Brigadier began to stir. 'It's all right, old friend.'

The Brigadier opened his eyes. 'Sorry, Headmaster,' he muttered deliriously, 'touch of vertigo. Won't happen again.' He blinked, and was suddenly wide awake. 'What the devil's been going on here?'

The Doctor grinned. This was more like the Brigadier of old. 'Quickly, Nyssa. Take the Brigadier to the TARDIS. Right into the centre and keep him there until I give the all-clear.' With a few words of encouragement to the confused Lethbridge-Stewart, he bundled them both out through the door.

The Doctor walked back to the regenerator control panel. 'Amazing – the Brigadier's timing. A millisecond either way and. . .'

'And what?'

'At the moment of exchange, the power didn't come from me, after all.'

'From the Brigadier?'

'From the TARDIS, really. Through the energy released by the Blinovitch Limitation Effect.'

'Can Nyssa and I time-travel?'

'You're as good as new.'

The Doctor was smiling confidently, and Tegan realised that, most important of all, he was still a Time Lord, with all his powers of regeneration intact.

They looked at the eight mutants. All were lying peacefully, as if asleep, the terrible blemishes gone from their bodies, a look of sublime calm suffusing each face.

'They're all dead,' said Tegan quietly.

'They would have travelled for the rest of time,' explained the Doctor. 'Death was all they wanted.' As he peered at Mawdryn's unravaged face, the mutant leader opened his eyes; the life had not entirely drained from him.

'It is finished, Doctor,' he whispered. He smiled a smile of utter contentment. 'Can this be . . . death?' His eyes closed, as his unfettered spirit soared to join his comrades, beyond the realms of time and space. It was the ending.

It was an exhausting business carrying the unconscious body of the younger (and thankfully lighter) Lethbridge-Stewart to the TARDIS. Half-way, Tegan and the Doctor had to stop for a rest.

'By the way,' said Tegan, suddenly very self-conscious. 'Thank you.'

'What?'

'You were prepared to give up everything for us.'

The Doctor just smiled and stood up. 'Oh, come on!'

Hardly had they begun to move again when they both came to a sudden halt. All around them the ship was beginning to creak and groan.

'The ship is dying with the mutants,' whispered the Doctor. 'Come on!' he shouted more urgently. 'It must be on auto-destruct.'

Jubilee Day, like the day of the Coronation itself, had been wet in the morning, but the clouds had rolled back by lunchtime, and the sun was shining brightly as Doctor Runciman climbed the hill to the obelisk. He wondered what on earth was the point of this mysterious rendezvous with Lethbridge-Stewart.

'Brigadier!' he shouted, as he reached the summit. 'Brigadier!'

Doctor Runciman walked off into the surrounding trees, and subsequently failed to see the blue police box materialise on the other side of the hilltop. By the time he returned from scouting the woods, the Doctor and Tegan had placed the unconscious Lethbridge-Stewart on the grass, and had returned to the TARDIS.

'Brigadier!' shouted Doctor Runciman, running towards the recumbent maths master.

The Brigadier groaned.

'Brigadier, what happened? I came as soon as I got your message.' He helped his patient to a sitting position. 'Brigadier, are you all right?'

Brigadier Lethbridge-Stewart stared straight ahead over Doctor Runciman's shoulder. He was still very dizzy, but could see the outline of what looked like a blue police box, which gradually . . . disappeared.

'My word, Doctor, you've been making a few changes in here!' The Brigadier, whom Nyssa had been keeping safe at the heart of the TARDIS, walked breezily into the control room.

'We all have to move with the times.' The Doctor smiled. 'How are you feeling?'

'Haven't felt so well for. . .' The Brigadier laughed. 'For six years, Doctor!' At last he understood the reason for his nervous breakdown. He breathed a sigh of relief.

Tegan was laughing too; this was more like the Brigadier she had met on her last visit to Brendon.

The Doctor indicated the flashing column. 'On our way to 1983. Back to school, Brigadier.'

The Brigadier smiled politely, as if a friendly travel agent had just offered special rates for a round trip on the *Titanic*, or Benton given him first refusal (special favour for you, sir) on some old lady's Morris Minor. If there had been a tram, a train or a Green Line bus, a dodgem car or a fairy cycle going in his direction, Lethbridge-Stewart would have taken it in preference to the Doctor's police box. (And Scotsman or no, paid full fare).

The Brigadier knew the TARDIS of old and, as the column slowed and stopped, he wondered where on Earth – or anywhere in the Universe – they were this time. The Doctor and the two girls escorted him to the door.

'Bless my soul!'

The sun was shining, it was a perfect summer's day, and the old house in the valley below was indubitably Brendon School. The Brigadier laughed. 'Goodbye, Doctor.' He shook his old friend by the hand. 'If ever you're passing. . .' The genial smile disappeared from his face. 'Where's Turlough?'

'Turlough!'

In all the excitement the boy had been entirely forgotten.

'He left in the capsule. . .' said the Doctor, trying to remember the complicated sequence of events.

'He can't have,' interrupted Nyssa. 'If the Brigadier was still on the ship, he never used the transmat capsule.'

'We've left him behind!' shouted Tegan, already

117

racing towards the TARDIS. 'Come on. That ship's on auto-destruct!'

The last thing Tegan expected to see as she rushed into the control room was Turlough. But there he was, leaning over the console, as if trying to set the co-ordinates.

'I'm hard to get rid of.' He smiled.

All Tegan's suspicions about the boy came flooding back. 'So it seems,' she replied icily.

'Turlough!' The Doctor was equally amazed to see the boy in the TARDIS.

Turlough looked at him somewhat quizzically for a second or two. 'May I join your crew, Doctor?'

'I think you already have,' said the Doctor.

It was quite normal for a pupil to disappear from Brendon School. Boys absconded; boys were expelled; boys were summoned to rejoin parents in Qatar and Addis Ababa; boys, these days, were even arrested. The Headmaster was remarkably unpeturbed to learn that Turlough had been removed. He was, however, only too relieved that nothing untoward had happened to the Brigadier. In fact, he couldn't remember when he last saw old Lethbridge-Stewart looking so well.

The Brigadier, wearing his Bursar's hat, assured the Headmaster that there was no question of Turlough's fees being refunded (all monies at Brendon payable in advance) and replied to Mr Sellick's observation on his excellent health that he felt like a new man.

There had been a message, waiting for him in the staff room, that a retired mechanic living in the village, had fallen in love with the vintage Humber languishing in the local garage, and had offered to put the old girl on the road again.

The Brigadier was quite bucked, and it was with a

light heart that he strolled, later that evening, down the lane to the Heskith Arms. He rather hoped Peter Runciman would look in before closing time; he'd like to buy the old boy a drink. The Brigadier began to whistle a little tune.

And far away, in the unhearing silence of space, the great red ship exploded into a million fragments.